CALEB'S SONG

Kathleen Ryder

DEDICATION

For Wyatt, with love.

PROLOGUE

The cool air hit Caleb like a slap across the cheek, he stumbled back, almost falling over an ill-placed garbage bin. His brother laughed, helped steady him, guided him carefully over to the carpark, buckling him in safely. It had been a good night, a long night. Caleb was glad Sam had come, it was easier to be himself when Sam was around, he didn't need to pretend to be someone else, didn't need to wear a mask of celebrity or pretentiousness. He could just be himself. Surprisingly, although there had been offers, neither of them was taking a woman home tonight. Oh well, there was always next time, and there would be a next time, Caleb was sure, this was their favourite Friday night haunt.

Laughing, Caleb turned to look at Sam, his eyes twinkling. "See," he couldn't help teasing the other man, "I knew you would have a good time tonight Sammy."

"I always have a good time with you little brother," Sam ruffled Caleb's perfectly lacquered hair, deliberately squashing the rock star 'ruffled just hopped straight out of bed' style that Caleb had spent hours perfecting earlier that night. "But we can't all be irresponsible rock stars now can we, Callie?" Sam used the childhood nickname he knew Caleb detested so much, knowing it would get a rise out of him. "Some of us actually

1

have to work to earn a living!" It was the same banter that always existed between them, the ribbing and poking fun that was laced with the love that comes from being part of a family.

"Work?!" snorted Caleb, "Ha! As if! You're a partner in a law firm Sammy, how much work can you possibly do? Don't you have a staff of people all waiting to jump to your command?" Caleb's raucous laugh mingled with Sam's deep chortle.

"Staff? That's your department brother dear, how many do you have now? Eighteen? Ninete-"

"Watch out!" Caleb's panicked shout interrupts Sam, and he blinks once, surprise etching his features. The unrelenting screech of bare metal tyre rims on bitumen reaches a crescendo before fading into silence, the world turning black, the only sound an incessant beep, beep, beep.

Caleb groaned as he rolled out of bed, ripping his alarm clock from the power socket, and pitching it across the room, cursing the sunlight streaming through the gap in the curtains as he did so. God, he hated mornings, or afternoons, or whatever horrid hour it happened to be. He ran a hand through his mop of brown hair, attempting, and failing, to untangle the knotted mess, before heading down the spiral staircase two at a time, in search of coffee. He didn't bother with a mug, chugging it straight from the percolator as he made his way through the open-plan middle level of his house, headed for the balcony that overlooked Darling Harbour.

Caleb had bought this house out of spite, a dumb spur of the moment decision that was his grown-up equivalent to sticking his tongue out at Sam. They had viewed this house together, Sam had joked that the house was a masterpiece of palatial proportions and that Caleb would never fill the sprawling statement in architectural mastery and design. He was right, Caleb had no intention of ever living in the breathtakingly luxurious family home, at least, not at first, not when he had bought it. The decision to move in, to actually reside here came later, after…Caleb shook his head to dispel the ghosts of a memory he could not, would not, address.

Located in one of Sydney's most privileged enclaves with sweeping elevated views over Darling Harbour, his home really was extraordinary from every angle. Spanning three incredible levels bathed in natural light, it boasted stunning French oak flooring, a gourmet kitchen, two spacious living areas and formal dining room, a butler's pantry, and a sun-soaked entertainers' terrace capturing magnificent views, while also overlooking the secluded level backyard with a swimming pool. There are six oversized bedrooms, all with their own ensuite, as well as an opulent master bedroom and luxurious ensuite featuring a sunken bath.

The expansive lower level included a nanny's quarters with a separate entrance, as well as a gym, home cinema, and extensive storage. There is underfloor heating and ducted air conditioning throughout the entire house, and two double lock-up garages plus off-street parking for three more cars. Apart from the bedroom he is using, and the kitchen, the only other room Caleb had spent much time in was the basement level, housing a wine cellar and a home studio. Although the house was purchased as a joke, Caleb had thought that he might use the studio one day. As it was, the most he had done was go down there and stare at the musical equipment as if he had no idea what to do with it, which, given his current state of mind, wasn't far off the truth.

He stared unseeing at the scene unfolding before him. A plane trailed across the sky, glinting against the blue horizon. Yachts skipped across the harbour, dancing a ballet with the passenger ferries. Crowds of people gathered at the world-famous Sydney Opera House, popular even when nothing was showing. The world around him was moving, people were living their lives as he watched on from his perch safely above it all. A frown marred Caleb's face. He could not remember when he had last left the house, there was no need. Anything he wanted was easily home delivered. No, he thought with disgust, that wasn't true. He knew when it was. The night he had taken Sam to a new nightclub opening, the world-famous bad boy Rockstar and his sensible older brother. They had been inseparable back then. Eleven months ago. A lifetime.

A week later Caleb had moved into this house, incognito. He made sure to email his parents, manager, and agent once a week, he didn't want them to worry any more than they already did about him. He knew he would have to see them soon, there was only so much healing time they would grant him, he knew their patience was wearing thin. Most days he really didn't care, but today, today was different. He wasn't ready to face them yet, or the media, he knew that, but he was restless, tired of being cooped up in an empty house with only himself for company. He needed to get away, out of this house, out of this whole wretched city with memories around every corner. Somewhere where no one knew him, where people would never even think to look for him.

An hour later, mind made up, Caleb strode out of his house, and tossed his duffel bag into the passenger seat of his Ferrari

488. He tore out of his driveway, foot down, only stopping for petrol once the city was a distant speck in his rear-view mirror.

CHAPTER ONE

"I'm sorry, we're fully booked out for the next two weeks." The clerk's chirpy response grated on Caleb's nerves.

"You're kidding!" Caleb looked around incredulously. This place was fully booked out?! No way could this brown and mustard sixties throwback colour scheme with the musty smell and vinyl high backed chairs be fully booked out. "I had no idea that Beryl Creek was such a tourist attraction," he commented dryly, feigning deafness at the incessant bleeping on his mobile phone. At least he wasn't too rural for wifi.

"It's the camel races this coming weekend, so," the young girl manning the desk shrugged nonchalantly, "yeah, like I said, fully booked out." Camel races, good grief, where on earth had he ended up? For the first time in seventy-two hours, Caleb started to wonder about his impulsive decision to leave. "You could always try the Bianchi place down the road, they sometimes take in guests when we are full," the clerk offered.

"The Bianchi's?"

"If you just drive straight down the main street, make a left turn at the only set of traffic lights, onto Finch Street. The last house on the left, with the white picket fence, is the Bianchi place." The only set of traffic lights? Interesting, this small town really was his version of hell, nothing less than he deserved, he thought wryly. With a final glance at the empty hotel lobby, Caleb turned and pushed through the exit doors. Two minutes later he was pulling up in front of the Bianchi house, a modest weatherboard, freshly painted white. He wondered if that was to match the fence or if the fence had come later. With a resigned sigh, he cut the engine and walked up the cobblestone path to the front porch. As he lifted his hand to knock on the front door, it swung open, bringing him face to face with a drooling horse.

"Bella, get down, you naughty dog." Huh, so not a horse then. "Mum, someone's at the door." A small face appeared around the side of the dog, a lopsided grin firmly in place. "Sorry about Bella, she won't hurt you, but she is a licker."

"Sofia honey, take Bella outside, you know Gramma doesn't like her in the house." Expressive sea blue eyes smiled around the corner. "Hi, I'm Gabby, can I help you?" Caleb shook her outstretched hand, smiling in spite of himself.

"Hi, I'm Caleb, I was sent here from the motel, I was hoping you had a room for rent?" Caleb didn't miss the once over that Gabby gave him, nor the unasked questions in her eyes.

"Of course, please," she gestured towards the open door, "won't you come in?" Caleb followed her through the small entryway into a spacious front room, doubling as a reception. While Gabby took out the reservation book Caleb took in his surroundings. This place was cosy, despite the openness of the room there was a real warmth here, it was a home, he realised nostalgically.

"How many nights were you looking to stay?" Gabby smiled up at him.

"Two weeks if possible," Caleb did a quick calculation. Yes, two weeks would do, it would see him past the one-year mark, if nothing else. Yes, he decided firmly, two weeks to sort out his sorry mess of a life and decide his future. It shouldn't be too hard to do, not in Beryl Creek in any case.

"We don't usually take-"

"Are you a gangster?" A small voice interrupted.

"Lucia!" Gabby gasped, jumping up from her chair behind the desk and crossing over to the small girl in the doorway. "No, he is not a gangster, why on earth would you even think such a thing? Go find Sofia, go on, and no bothering Grampa." Her tone held a warning. "I'm sorry," she turned towards Caleb, "school holidays have just started, and the girl's grandfather likes to regale them with stories of his youth," she smiled fondly. "Not that he was a gangster," she hastened to add, "he was a police officer," she finished lamely.

Caleb laughed, he knew he shouldn't, but he just could not help himself. The embarrassed look on her face was priceless. "I'm sorry," he gasped out, "really, I am. It's just that I have never been mistaken for a gangster before." A bastard, yes, cruel and unfeeling, sure, but never an actual villain. He was surprised to find himself laughing, he had almost forgotten what it sounded like.

"Perhaps it is the full black ensemble?" A smile tugged at the corners of Gabby's mouth. "Come on, let me show you the room and then you can decide if it will be suitable or not." Caleb followed Gabby up a curved staircase to a second-floor landing, housing an overstuffed bookcase and several pot plants, and down a narrow hallway with several doors leading off it. She leads him to the door furthest away from the landing, and fishing a key out of her pocket, unlocks the door. The room is large, tastefully decorated in whites and greys, polished wooden floorboards. A king-sized bed sits in the middle of the room, a large window opens out over the garden, allowing a soft breeze to waft in. A small round table and chairs, and a wardrobe housing a TV, kettle, and bar fridge complete the room. A second door leads off into a small ensuite.

"It's perfect, I'll take it."

"Excellent," Gabby beamed up at him, "if you'll follow me, we'll get the paperwork sorted out and then I will send up some afternoon tea Mister...." Gabby trailed off, looking up at him expectantly.

"Mr Roman," Uh, oh. Here it comes. "Caleb Roman." Caleb held his breath, watching Gabby intently. Huh, nothing, not even a flicker of recognition. Maybe he will be okay here after all, maybe he will have the peace he craves.

"Well, welcome to Beryl Creek Caleb", Gabby smiled at him before leading him back downstairs and through to the office. Ten minutes later, paperwork sorted, suitcase stashed at the base of the wardrobe, Caleb flopped down on the bed, feet dangling off the edge, and stared at the ceiling. He fished out his mobile phone from his pocket, and without reading any of them, deleted all of his messages, before switching his phone off and tossing it in the direction of the door. He could feel the stress of the drive ebbing away, weariness settling around him like a fog, eyes heavy, his last conscious thought was that of a small child's whisper on the wind.

When Caleb woke it was to a room streaked with the dawn, muffled sounds drifting up from below. The illuminated numbers on the bedside clock surprised him, confused him momentarily. While he used to be able to live the rockstar life of partying until dawn and sleeping until noon, he never slept through the night anymore, hadn't for almost twelve months now. In fact, he considered himself lucky if he managed to get five hours of sleep a night. Yet here he was, fully clothed, pins and needles from sleeping on his hand, shoes still on from yesterday. If the clock was to be believed, he had slept without stirring, without being plagued by dreams of a past best forgotten, for fifteen hours. He sat up, stretching arms high above his head, absently wondering what brand of bed he had slept on and whether he should get one for his house or not. He crossed the room to flick on the light switch, noticing a sign on the wall beside it. Guest rules. Huh, he had never been particularly good at following the rules.

He skimmed the list quickly. Rule number one is no smoking inside. Okay, that he could do, never having taken up that particular vice. Rule number two, no drugs. Again, not an issue for him. Rule number three, no overnight guests. Hmm, that one would usually have been far trickier, but aside from being in a dinky country town with severely limited options, he had been having somewhat of a dry spell lately. A fact that should have upset him but didn't, not that he wanted to analyse why that was either. Below the rules were the hours meals were served, Caleb was relieved to see breakfast was only half an hour away, he was ravenous! Padding through to the ensuite, Caleb showered, the water banishing the last traces of sleep. As he reached for a tee-shirt to pull on, he stilled, a smile quirking at the side of his lips as he looked down at himself, remembering yesterday's assessment of resembling a gangster. Black sneakers, his trademark skinny black jeans, and now, in his hand, a crumpled black tee shirt. Huh, he really did need to expand his colour choices. He threw the tee shirt back in his suitcase and rifled around some more, eventually locating and settling on a slate grey one instead, before closing his door behind him and heading downstairs in search of the dining room.

CHAPTER TWO

The scent reached him halfway down the stairs, enveloping him, making his mouth water. He wasn't sure what to expect from the dining room, having only ever stayed in the finest hotels and partaking in their room service, but he was pretty sure this was not standard. The modest-sized dining room held an oval table in the centre, with seating for twelve. A buffet table ran the length of one wall and laden down with all manner of sinfully delicious treats. Plates of decadent chocolate filled pastries, thick slices of fruit toast, and miniature custard tartlets vied with dishes of fluffy scrambled eggs, plump little chipolatas, and golden hash browns. His stomach growled appreciatively, a blush creeping up his neck as five pairs of eyes turned, mid-conversation, to look at him.

"Caleb, good morning." Gabby greeted him with a smile, "grab a plate and help yourself, you must be starving." He did as she suggested, piling his plate with an embarrassing amount of food while she busied herself with refilling coffee cups.

"Did you sleep well? We weren't sure whether or not to wake you for dinner, and in the end, we decided that you obviously needed the sleep." Caleb slid into the chair Gabby indicated. "Let me introduce you to everyone. These are my parents, Maria and Nico," she indicated an older couple at the head of the table. The woman was plump, her face was guarded, showed signs of strain, and Caleb had no trouble imagining her wielding a rolling pin aloft at anyone who dared to go against her. The man was hunched in on himself, and

Caleb wondered if he was warm enough. His face was friendly, open, and Caleb knew he would be quick to laugh. Caleb was surprised to see him in a wheelchair, how did he manage the stairs? "And these little monkeys are Lucia and Sofia," she waved her hand towards two little girls currently giggling behind their hands. The resemblance was eerie.

"Twins?"

"Yes," Gabby replied offhandedly, adding butter and condiments to the lazy Susan in the centre of the table. "But please don't worry," Gabby graced him with a smile, "they won't bother you while you are staying with us, I promise."

"Bother him?" Maria spoke, indignation tinting her voice. "How can you say that? These two, nothing but goodness, that's what they are."

"Mother," Gabby's tone held a clear warning, Lucia and Sofia scooted closer to each other, watching the scene warily.

"Maria, she didn't mean anything by it, come on now, eat your breakfast, you know Gabby made those pastries for you," Nico placated his wife with a broad grin, adding his own pastry to her plate. "It is nice to have you here Caleb, tell me, what is it that you do?" Uh oh, Caleb hadn't actually thought about his profession. Should he tell them the truth? No, the last thing he needed was for the wretched paparazzi to find him here, especially when he was this close to twelve months. No, besides, after two weeks he wouldn't see any of them again, so a little white lie wouldn't hurt, would it?

"I own a music shop." Not exactly a lie, he and Sam did buy a music shop, not that he ever spent any time there, his face was far too recognisable to work in a shop. Still, it remained a solid investment and a base for him to use for CD signings and press conferences.

"A music shop, how wonderful! Do you play?"

"I've played the guitar for twenty years or so. My dad thought it would keep me out of trouble as a teen." Laughter tinged Caleb's reply at the memory.

"And did it?"

"It certainly cemented my direction in life, that is for sure." Caleb took a swig of coffee. "I also play the piano and the viola, although nowhere near the level at which I play the guitar".

"Did you bring your guitar with you?" Sofia, or was it Lucia, piped up. "Maybe you can play for us?" Uh oh, not where he wanted this conversation to go at all.

"I brought one of them with me yes," he hoped that would be the end of their innocent questions.

"How many guitars do you have Mr Roman?"

"I have over three hundred," Caleb smiled proudly. "I like to collect guitars from all over the world, I have them in storage now, and some of them are at my shop, but one day I want to have a special room just to display them in."

"That would be awesome!" Yes, Caleb thought, it sure would be. "So, will you play for us, puh-lease?"

"I'm sorry, but no, I can't," he cleared his throat self-consciously. "I, ah, was in an accident a while ago, I can't play." He was unable to hide the way his hand shook as he held his coffee cup, clattered it into the saucer before he dropped it. His anguished voice left no room for argument, he loathed how vulnerable it made him sound, like a weak coward. That's what he was, weak.

"Well," Maria looked at him gently, "what you need is a nice stay in the country, no? Two weeks with us, you'll see, you'll play again." She nodded her head vigorously. "Beryl Creek is magic; did you know that? This town was named for Beryl

Rossi, my great great grandmother. She was a witch, a healer, this town protected her when no one else would, and in return, she blessed the townsfolk with the creek that runs through the centre of town. Mark my words, you'll see, there is magic in the air, and in the water, here." Caleb smiled, it was a nice idea in any case, and obviously meant to comfort him.

"Thank you, I look forward to that," he was surprised to realise that he actually meant the words he spoke.

"Well then, it's settled. Gabby, you and the girls can show Caleb around Beryl Creek after work this afternoon". If Gabby disagreed with her mother ordering her to show him around, and it was most definitely an order, she certainly didn't show it.

"You work?" Too late Caleb realised how incredulous that sounded, and not wanting to cause offence, he hastened to add, "I'm sorry, I meant…I thought running the bed and breakfast was your full-time job," he finished lamely.

"No," Gabby drained her coffee cup, "Mum and dad own the bakery in town, I work there. Baker, shop girl, accountant, you name it, I do it." She stood, kissing the girls on their cheeks, "I better go, Mr Porter will be wondering where his bread is." She shared a secret smile with her dad. "You girls be good for nanna and poppy today, stay out of Mr Roman's way. When I get home, we'll walk up to town. If poppy says you've been good, we'll get ice cream for dessert." Her statement was met with a loud cheer from the girls, and Caleb suspected that their poppy would say they had been good even if they burnt the house down.

After breakfast had been finished, Caleb allowed the girls to show him where the garden was, a lush green oasis brimming with butterflies and the sounds of birds calling out a greeting to each other. Tucked neatly into the far corner of the garden was a white wooden cubby house, complete with a covered veranda, and cheerful bunting hanging from the guttering, swaying in the gentle summer breeze. A well-tended tiered vegetable garden ran the entire length of the back yard, vines laden down with passionfruit obscured the fence from view, pumpkin tendrils snaked across the lawn, and tomatoes spilled from stakes. A giant peppercorn tree partially hid the house from view, covering the lush green lawn with shade. Potted flowers and herbs filled the undercover back patio, a riot of colours and smells assaulted his senses. It was, he decided, an oasis, a soothing balm to the ugliness of the world outside. Feeling unusually inspired, Caleb retrieved a notebook and pen from his room upstairs, dragging a lawn chair into the shade of the old peppercorn tree, sitting to stare up through its waterfall of branches at the patches of cloudless blue sky overhead.

Warm summer air mingled with a gentle breeze, fluttering across his face. He wasn't sure how long he stayed there, staring, unseeing, at the dreamy azure while images, unbidden, danced behind his eyelids. Memories of another time and place, a laugh frozen in time, a future unrealised. Sighing heavily, he picked up his pen and started to sketch out the start of a new song, a few lines of disjointed lyrics that he would attempt to weave together into something coherent later. They were dreadful, amateurish. He was woefully out of practice, whereas before he would have been able to string together the lyrics for an award-winning song in minutes and compose it by the end of the day. It wasn't that he didn't want to write exactly, it was just that he was conflicted. He didn't want to inflict his deep-seated anguish and pain, or worse, his self-loathing, onto any of his fans via his music, which is exactly what he feared would happen if he wrote anything new now. It was all he had left, it that he had within himself now, a gaping blackness. He wasn't sure he wanted to return to his old self, didn't know if he could. It surprised him to realise that it didn't bother him as much as it would have previously. Maybe music wasn't his future anymore, maybe he was done with that whole scene.

The question was, if he gave it up, what would he do? More importantly, who would he be? Music had been his identity for eighteen years; he had gotten his big break when he was seventeen, and the band he formed in his father's garage had opened for the Sydney Music Festival. Unheard of for an unknown band, they had been lucky, the original band scheduled had needed to pull out, the organiser's assistant had just heard Caleb's song on a demo. A week later, their lives had changed. Caleb was proud of the fact that all of the original band members were still active in the band, and more importantly, still the best of friends. At least, they had been. Caleb wasn't sure if they would forgive him this year of silence, apart from an occasional email or text message, Caleb had intentionally ignored them. Self-absorbed and selfish, his inner voice chided him, not in the least bit flattering these days.

His inner voice, his constant companion, urging him to do better, to be better, the one voice Caleb had been unable to tune out, no matter how he tried.

CHAPTER THREE

He sat, stringing lyrics and poems together, until the shadows darkened, closed in around him, the air stilling. A dog barked off in the distance, calling for his supper, a car engine cut out, the screen door slammed, excited voices grew louder as they approached him

"Mister Roman?" Tentative, not sure if it should intrude on his solitude. Caleb stood, dragging his chair out from under the peppercorn tree, smiling down at Sofia and Lucia. "Mama's home, she said if you wanted to, we will show you around the town?"

"Hmm," Caleb pretended to think about the question. "Will there be ice cream?"

"Uh-huh," serious brown eyes met his, "poppy told mama we were very good."

"Then let's go." A flurry of excited chatter drowned out anything else that Caleb might have said, and he dutifully followed the girls inside, only managing to catch half of what it was they were saying. He left them waiting in the lounge room while he dashed upstairs for his wallet, stopping short when he heard his name mentioned.

"I didn't make them for Caleb dad, I made them for you." A cajoling laugh had Caleb wondering just what Gabby had made.

"You should be baking for a husband, not an old man." A heavy sigh.

"Dad," a warning.

"What? I can't have an opinion now? Gabby, you shouldn't be here, caring for a cripple. You're wasting your life." Regret mingled with sadness, Caleb wondered what had happened to Nico to colour his tone.

"Dad, enough! You are not a burden to me, stop talking like this, please. Now, are you sure that you want to stay up here while the girls and I are out? I'm happy to ca-"

"No, I'll be fine, I know you're tired."

"I'll bring you back some butterscotch swirl ice cream; we won't be back late." Not wanting to get caught eavesdropping, Caleb slipped quietly into his room and slowly counted to one hundred, returning to the lounge room just after Gabby.

The walk into the centre of town took longer than Caleb thought it would, considering it was only two blocks away. Both Lucia and Sofia were keen to point out all of their favourite objects to him. Honestly, he had never seen so many trees given such peculiar attributes before. He had to admit though, their imaginations were delightful. He wondered if he had been this imaginative as a child, he made a mental note to ask his mum the next time he spoke to her. If there was a next time, he thought guiltily, aware of the fact that after twelve months with barely a hello, she may, in fact, relegate him to the doghouse once he finally returned to Sydney and started taking her calls again. The familiar ache throbbed in his chest, nostalgia for childhood and a longing for the comfort of home, of his mother's embrace, rose up, robbing him of his breath. He swallowed hard, forcing the feeling aside, not prepared to dissect it right now.

As with most federation towns, Beryl Creek celebrated its heritage, with all of the shops along the main street retaining their quaint antique facades. In some cases, a single business was spread through two or three shop fronts, an interior wall knocked out to create a larger space. As far as main streets went, this one was postcard-perfect, or it would have been had it not been bustling with jostling tourists. Although Beryl Creek was nothing more than a mere blip on a map, Caleb discovered it was surprisingly bigger than it looked. Beryl Creek, Gabby informed him, boasted a newsagency, ice cream parlour, butcher, veterinarian, fruit shop, medical centre, large corner store, motel, takeaway shop, caravan park, florist, two pubs, three churches, and, a bakery.

They wandered up one side of the main street, Gabby pointing out bits of interesting trivia and town lore as they went, stopping several times as people chatted to Gabby, asking after her parents. It was obvious the town felt very highly of the older couple. As promised, their first stop was the ice cream parlour, the elaborate gold-lettered Edwardian sign proclaiming it to be Aunt Vi's Ice Cream Parlour. Caleb could see why the girls were so eager to come here, it was a child's dream world. Old fashioned booths ran down the entire middle of the store, with the side wall covered in a dizzying array of candy, in a riot of colours that wouldn't have looked out of place in a boutique store in Sydney. An old-fashioned counter ran the length of the opposite wall, with glass cases displaying the various ice creams on offer. Lucia and Sofia ran ahead, eagerly pushing their faces up to the glass, oohing and aahing over the flavours.

"They love seeing Vi's latest crazy creation," Gabby offered as she and Caleb made their way over to the girls."

"Gabby! It is so good to see you hun, how you doin'?" The scent of freshly cut carnations swirled around Caleb's head as strong arms embraced Gabby across the countertop.

"Aunty Vi, you saw me at lunchtime," Gabby teased.

"Well now, a lot can happen in a few hours, can't it?" Vi looked pointedly at Caleb.

"Aunt Vi! Seriously, this is Caleb, a guest at our bed and breakfast." The shocked rebuttal was a knee jerk reaction, Caleb was sure, but still…He felt stirrings of indignation at the speed at which Gabby dismissed her Aunt's thinly veiled suggestion. Honestly, he was a catch, there were scores of women around the world all eager to be able to claim they had spent even a single night in bed with the famous Caleb Roman, let alone…Huh. The thought brought him up short. Perhaps all of him hadn't turned to stone that night, after all, interesting.

They ordered their ice cream cones and took them outside, wandering slowly towards the creek that the town drew its name from.

"Caleb, I'm sorry for back there," Gabby worried her bottom lip. "I realise that probably sounded rude, but Vi is the biggest gossip in Beryl Creek. She either cajoles your secret out of you herself, or she simply makes something up. I've, ah, learnt to set her straight over the years."

"Thanks for the heads up," Caleb was unable to resist teasing her. "I think I had better steer clear of her while I am in town then, I wouldn't want her discovering my deep dark secrets."

"Puh-leeze," Gabby snorted, "how many could you possibly have?" Indeed, thought Caleb, swallowing down the bile rising in his throat. If only she knew.

They finished their ice creams in companionable silence, perched on a boulder, watching the girls splash by the edge of the river. As the sun started to set, and the shadows grew longer, Gabby rose, brushed the few stray crumbs from her floral dress, and called for the girls. There was a chorus of complaints, a verbal protest at the fairness of going home at this early hour, only silenced with the promise that they would be allowed to remain up past their bedtime once they got home, in order to watch a DVD. They made a final stop at Aunt Vi's Ice Cream Parlour, Caleb offering to remain outside with the girls while Gabby went in, returning shortly with a tub of butterscotch ice cream for her father, and two bags of old fashioned mixed lollies for the girls. The walk home was silent, each engrossed in their own thoughts and plans. Once home, the girls rushed upstairs to give their poppy his ice cream, and to tell him all about their adventures.

Gabby walked through to the kitchen, taking out plates and a various assortment of grocery items, mixing and whipping and chopping, humming softly to herself as she went.

"Caleb, would you mind setting the table, please? There are plates in that cupboard there," Gabby gestured broadly in Caleb's direction. "Just four, mum and dad will eat upstairs tonight." Caleb did as he was asked, watching Gabby as she moved about. "Simple pizza for dinner tonight, I hope you don't mind?"

"Are you kidding?! I love a good pizza."

"Mama's pizzas aren't 'good', they are the best in the world!" a small voice piped up, Lucia and Sofia sidling up to Gabby.

"Is that so?" Caleb teased.

"Yep." Heads nodded vigorously, the confidence of youth.

"Well, in that case, I can't wait to try it."

CHAPTER FOUR

An hour later, full of Capricciosa pizza, garlic bread, and green salad, Caleb leant back on his pillows and groaned. The girls had been right, that had been the best pizza he had ever eaten. After dinner the girls had been given their bags of candy and settled in the lounge room to watch their DVD, their nanna coming down to join them. Caleb had offered to help Gabby with the dishes and had dried while she washed, keeping up a steady stream of conversation, enjoying listening to the sound of her voice. It was warm caramel, soothing to his aching soul, dangerously addictive. The realisation had him bidding her good night and retiring to his room. He had found the entire evening more fun than he would have thought, it was a nice change from his usual frozen dinner for one eaten straight out of the packet while standing at the kitchen bench. An unhealthy habit he knew but alienating everyone in his life had made him realise just how awful he was at actually cooking anything other than toast. Now that was something that he could change. Reaching for his laptop he opened up an internet browser ad navigated to a search engine. Within a few clicks, he had found a cooking school close to his home and shot them off an email enquiring about private classes.

The fresh air from his walk combined with the fullness from a home-cooked meal soon had Caleb's eyelids drooping, and for the second night in a row, he fell asleep fully clothed.

Laughing, Caleb turned to look at Sam, his eyes twinkling. "See," he couldn't help teasing the other man, "I knew you would have a good time tonight Sammy."

"I always have a good time with you little brother," Sam ruffled Caleb's perfectly lacquered hair, deliberately squashing the rock star 'ruffled fresh from bed' style that Caleb had spent hours perfecting earlier that night. "But we can't all be irresponsible rockstars now can we, Callie?" Sam used the childhood nickname he knew Caleb detested so much, knowing it would get a rise out of him. "Some of us actually have to work to earn a living!" It was the same banter that always existed between them, the ribbing and poking fun that was laced with the love that comes from being part of a family.

"Work?!" snorted Caleb, "Ha! As if! You're a partner in a law firm Sammy, how much work can you possibly do? Don't you have a staff of people all waiting to jump to your command?" Caleb's raucous laugh mingled with Sam's deep chortle.

"Staff? That's your department brother dear, how many do you have now? Eighteen? Ninete-"

"Watch out!" Caleb's panicked shout interrupts Sam, and he blinks once, surprise etching his features. The unrelenting screech of bare metal tyre rims on bitumen reaches a crescendo before fading into silence, the world turning black.

Caleb moaned softly, pain radiating from his shoulder. He squeezed his eyes shut tight, then opened them, blinking rapidly until the interior of the car stopped swirling in front of him. He turned his head slightly, eyes searching in the half-light for Sam. Where was he? Opening his door with momentous effort, Caleb hauled himself into an upright position, ignoring the trickle of blood running down his face, waving away the concerned faces hovering in front of him. He looked around, why was everyone moving so slowly? Gabby was standing at the edge of the road, watching him, smiling in expectation. Lucia and Sofia stood next to her, waving at him. What were they doing here? Where was Sam?

Caleb turned towards the small crowd that had gathered in the middle of the road, a short distance behind the car. Everyone was out of focus, nothing made sense. Did someone drug him in the club? Sam should be here. He looked down, his hands were covered in blood, so much blood. He blinked, looked down at the road, saw Sam's sneakers sticking out from the crowd gathered. Funny, Caleb didn't remember moving. The crowd parted, Sam laid on the road, hands linked behind his head, a boyish smile etched onto his face.

"Sam, what are you doing, this is a road, you can't stay here, we'll be late."

"Look at the stars little brother," Sam flicked his hand in the direction of the night sky. "You're a star, you know that right? You're translucendal Cal, translucendal." Sam drew the last word out, slowly enunciating every single syllable.

"What are you talking about," Caleb's voice sounded so far away, even to his own ears. "That not even a word Sam, you just made it up."

"I'm pretty sure it's a word little brother, and if not, it should be." Sam smiled up at Caleb. "It's what you are, Caleb, don't forget that. Translucendal."

"Sam, enough," Caleb frowned, consternation etching his features. "Why are you lying here? What are we doing, come on, we need to go."

"Cal." Sam only called him that when he was being serious, which was a rare thing. "We are already here."

"What are you talking about, you're not making any sense."

"Don't you remember Cal? You killed me. You ran us off the road with your incessant chatter about your own self-importance. I died Cal, a slow and painful death because you had to be a star".

Caleb sat bolt upright, drenched in sweat. Great, the nightmares again. He padded across to the ensuite and flicked on the light, catching sight of himself in the mirror. With a grimace, he rubbed his hand over his tired face. He looked like hell. Worse than that, he felt like hell. The nightmares plagued him, daylight offered no relief, the images on a constant loop in his head. He wondered, as he did in every moment of the day, if nightmare Sam was right. Was he too wrapped up in his own self-importance? Not that it mattered anymore, nothing mattered anymore. He just needed to get through the next two weeks, that was all, after that, he was sure he would be fine. Maybe.

Treading carefully, Caleb silently made his way down the hallway, feeling rather like a teenager sneaking home past curfew, hoping not to wake anyone. He reached the bottom step and was just crossing to the front door when a hand snaked out and touched his forearm, nearly sending him through the roof.

"What the hell?!" Caleb all but screeched, voice a couple of octaves higher than usual. Smooth, real smooth, he thought to himself with disgust.

"I'm sorry, I didn't mean to scare you." The teasing glint in her eyes said something else. "There are warm cinnamon scrolls on the kitchen bench if you wanted some before you go out." Gabby opened the front door, paused, turned, and grinned. "And just so you know, the back stairs are much better for sneaking out, they squeak less."

"Thanks, I'll keep that in mind." Sprung! "What about you, do you make it a habit of baking cinnamon scrolls in the middle of the night?"

"It's three o'clock in the morning Caleb, hardly the middle of the night, and yes actually. I am usually up by two o'clock most mornings, once I finish the pastries for the house, I head over to the bakery to start prep for the day. What's your excuse?"

"Bad dream," Caleb muttered, shuffling his feet back and forth.

"I'm sorry," Gabby fixed him with a hard stare. "I know how they can haunt a person. My father…Well, anyway, I better go, have fun on your adventures today."

"Wait, can I come with you?" The words were out before he had a chance to think his request through, he wanted to kick himself. What on earth had he been thinking, asking to go with her? To where? Work of all places. To do what, watch her? Good grief, he must really be desperate for some human interaction, either that or he was still dreaming. She was watching him now, eyebrows knitted together, a perplexed look on her face.

"Um, sure, if you want to, but I must warn you, it's not terribly exciting." She gave him an out, he should have taken it. Instead, his mouth opened, surprising them both with his reply.

"Lead the way."

CHAPTER FIVE

"So, this is it, the famous bakery." Caleb smiled as he looked around, it was pretty much as he had imagined it would look, tastefully decorated as if it was an extension of the Bianchi house.

"This is it. Come on, I'll show you what needs to happen." Caleb followed her through to the kitchen, a spacious stainless-steel affair, stopping when she pointed something out to him. "This is today's list."

"You do all this? Who helps you?" There had to be fifty items on her list.

"We don't employ anyone else, I do the baking, selling, cleaning, whatever needs doing. Mum and dad watch the girls during the day if it is school holidays, otherwise, they come here after school and help out".

"That seems like a lot of work for just one person," Caleb frowned. "Why don't you employ a staff? It would make life a lot easier for you, and you would get more time with the girls too, which I am guessing you would like."

"Mister Roman," uh oh, he knew that tone all too well, she was angry with him. "I brought you here today because you asked to come. As a guest in my parent's bed and breakfast, I didn't see any harm in you seeing how our Italian bakery operates, it supplies half the town, and the methods we use are old school traditional. However, please do not think that by bringing you here, you have the right to question how I run this bakery. Because you do not!" Her eyes flashed a warning, a crimson flush creeping up her neck.

"I'm sorry", Caleb had the grace to look chagrined. "That was rude, forgive me. I know it's no excuse, it is just that, well…I have staff." Caleb shrugged. "To be honest I never really thought about it until recently, but they make my life easier in so many ways. I just wondered…" He cleared his throat awkwardly.

"We can't afford to hire anyone, let's leave it at that."

Caleb felt bad. After their earlier argument, Gabby had been frosty with him. It was nothing less than he deserved, he knew that, still, he felt bad. He had tried to make amends by attempting to make them both a strong coffee from the space-age barista machine on the front counter, but after somehow exploding a stream of steaming hot milk from the top of the frother, volcano style, Gabby had asked him to simply grab some juice from the fridge. At least that was something he could manage without disaster.

"Can I help you with that?" He didn't miss the wary look she gave him over the mixer, hastening to add, "I mean, ah, if you show me how, I would love to learn how to do that."

"Have you ever actually baked before Caleb?"

"Mum never used to like us kids in the kitchen," he admitted sheepishly, earning an eyebrow quirk from Gabby.

"I wonder why?" She teased dryly, before a soft sigh escaped her lips. "Sure, why not," a shoulder shrug. "What could go wrong?" Caleb hoped that was a rhetorical question.

The bakery looked as if a bomb had gone off, which, to be honest, wasn't very far from the truth, Gabby thought wryly to herself. There was flour from one end of the kitchen to the other, she had eggshell in her hair, and, there was a very distinct blob of chocolate mousse on the ceiling. Urgh, it was going to be a very long day. How was it possible for someone to be so very bad in the kitchen? Caleb, she decided, was a walking disaster. She could only imagine what life had been like for his poor mother, no wonder she refused to let him into the kitchen.

"If my mum could see me now, she would die from the shock," Caleb joked, proudly admiring the rather sad looking cupcake sitting in front of him. "It's not too bad for a first effort, is it?" Pride laced with vulnerability had always been Gabby's weakness and she crossed to him, slinging her arm loosely across his back, squeezing lightly.

"No, Caleb, for a first effort, it is pretty impressive." She was stopped from saying anything else by the gentle tapping on the front glass door.

"Mrs Porter, good morning, come on in."

"Gabby, thank you, dear, I know you aren't actually open yet, but I saw the light on in the front and thought I would, oh!" She stopped, spying Caleb. "I'm sorry, I didn't realise you had company, I can come back later."

"Mrs Porter, this is Caleb, a house guest at the bed and breakfast."

"Caleb, gosh, you're quite handsome, aren't you? He reminds me of those rock stars you see on the TV nowadays." Caleb blushed uncomfortably. It would be just his luck, to be recognised in a small town by this old lady.

"Mrs Porter?" Gabby pushed gently.

"Hmm, oh yes dear, of course. It's Bert, he was up again last night, I thought perhaps one of your custard pies might cheer him up a bit."

"Of course, I'll bag one up, and your usual bread?" Gabby led Mrs Porter out to the counter, voices fading away. Gabby's warm laugh, the tinkling of the bell over the door signifying Mrs Porter's departure, the scratching of a chair on the tiles next to him.

"Come on chef, we open in an hour, let's get this mess cleaned up."

"Now that," he grinned at her, "is something I excel at. Here," he pushed her towards the kitchen stool, "you sit, I will clean."

"Done." It was nice, Gabby decided, watching someone else do the cleaning for a change, especially when that someone else was as good looking as Caleb was. Yummy! Her tongue darted out across her lips, subconsciously, longingly. He was an enigma, a puzzle to be solved. He was obviously wealthy, she wasn't an idiot, that car he drove had to be worth hundreds of thousands of dollars. Plus, he said he had staff, and yet, he knew how to clean, thoroughly, professionally.

"What is it?" Caleb turned, feeling eyes on the back of his head, surprising Gabby mid appraisal.

"I was, ah, just trying to figure you out, that's all." A blush, interesting. Perhaps there was a chance rule number three, no overnight guests, would be needed after all.

"Don't try too hard."

"Is that an order?" She tried to make light of the suddenly dark tone of Caleb's voice.

"Consider it a warning, that's all."

"Better the devil I know, and all that?"

"Exactly." Caleb nodded his agreeance.

"Are you the devil Caleb?" The softness of her voice floated around him, fogging his brain, clouding his judgement. Dropping the cloth he was using, he was by her side in two strides, arms resting on the counter either side of her, trapping her. His face was dangerously close to hers; he saw her pupils dilate, felt her breath hitch. Her scent enveloped him, he was in trouble, he knew that, and yet…He just could not resist the pull, had to know what her lips felt like on his, how they tasted. He closed the gap between them painstakingly slowly, giving her every chance to change her mind, silently willing her to do so.

"Would you like me to be?"

He captured her mouth in a single move, felt her moan beneath him as she melted into him. The tip of his tongue pressed against her lips, seeking admission, rejoicing when she gave it willingly, sighing against him. His hand snaked through her hair, angling her head to deepen their kiss. He was drowning in her, lost in a sea of vanilla and nutmeg, no longer sure of where he ended and she began. Needing, aching, to be closer, he gripped her waist, lifting her onto the bench. Her slender legs wound around his waist instinctively, urging him closer, her hands tangled in his hair. He could feel the roundness of her curves against his chest, sliding a hand up the arch of her back and around to cup her breast. He weighed it in his hand, pinching at the nipple through the fabric of her dress, earning a cry of pleasure as it pebbled beneath his touch.

"Caleb," she broke their kiss, gasping his name. "Oh yes, yes, please," she guided his mouth to her breast, "don't stop. Please." It was the pleading that pulled him up short.

He should have known better than to kiss her, that kiss weakened him everywhere. His shaky breath, the hardness of his arousal. God he wanted her, wanted to bury himself deep inside her softness, to taste her, to discover what would make her scream his name. He ached to be the reason that she came undone, but he wouldn't be. He would not, could not, do that to her, not when he was only staying for two weeks, and had nothing to offer beyond that. He saw the confusion in her eyes, the unasked questions, the embarrassment.

"Gabby," his voice husky with desire, "I can't, I'm sorry." He pushed himself away from the bench, taking her with him, steadying her before letting go completely. "It's not that I don't want to, believe me, I want to," he gestured to the bulge in his trousers, evidence of just how much he wanted her. "I just can't. Not here, not like this." He lifted her chin, fixing her with a devilish smile. "When I take you to bed Gabby, and it will happen, I promise, it won't be here, where someone could interrupt us. When I make love to you, I intend to take my time, for both of us."

Gabby's head spun. What on earth had she been thinking, kissing Caleb? Kissing anyone for that matter. Stupid, stupid, stupid! That's what she had been, stupid, especially after Michael. She was angry with herself, she thought she had learnt her lesson, thought she had become smarter. She touched her lips gently, swollen with want. She still wanted him, Caleb, she could still feel his mouth on hers, the realisation confusing her. Thank heavens her mother hadn't been here to witness her moment of weakness; it would have been just one more disappointment in a long line of disappointing daughter moments that she relished pulling out and using to her advantage whenever it suited her. Despite their shared kiss, or maybe because of it, Gabby was acutely aware of Caleb's every move throughout the day. The way he spoke to the customers, including them and listening to them as if they were old friends, warmed her heart. Michael never did that. Actually, Michael had only ever set foot in the bakery when he had no other choice, thinking it beneath him, all the manual labour and shopkeeping.

Gabby shook her head to clear the cobwebs of the ghosts that had long resided there. Michael was another lifetime ago, there was no use in rehashing the past, or in hoping for anything for the future. She needed to focus on the present, that was all. She would not let anyone turn her head again, especially not someone who wouldn't be here in three weeks. No, she had learnt the hard way, the only person to depend on was herself. This attraction to Caleb was just lust, that was all. Nothing more than that. She would easily forget all about him, she was a Bianchi for heaven's sake, she had willpower by the bucketful. She just had to find it.

CHAPTER SIX

The rest of the afternoon passed slowly, Gabby felt as if she were swimming through treacle, her limbs were heavy, sluggish. Every fibre of her being was acutely aware of Caleb, as if she had been placed into some sort of trance, unable to form coherent thoughts anymore, her brain a mess of cotton wool. He, on the other hand, looked completely at ease, not a hair out of place. How can he be so collected while she is a dithering mess? Maybe he makes it a habit of his, kissing girls senseless, Gabby's inner critic baited her. He didn't look like that type of man though, and when he had kissed her, he seemed almost unsure of himself, as if he hadn't kissed anyone in a long time. Gabby frowned, why was she defending him, even to herself? It made no difference to her, she had no intention of getting involved with him, she shrugged slightly, none at all.

Closing time could not come soon enough, as Gabby flipped the door sign from open to close, she honestly could not wait to get home and have a glass of Chianti Classico.

"Well, I bet you got more than you bargained for today Caleb," the words were out before she could stop them, a deep blush creeping up her neck and fanning across her face. "I mean, with the offer of helping out. We were busier than usual, probably because the camel races are on in a few days," she mused.

"It was my pleasure," he chuckled softly, "oh, and Gabby," he turned from the bench he was wiping down to look at her fully, "I meant what I said, next time, there will be no interruptions," a slow smile curled across Caleb's face, his gaze travelled lazily down Gabby's body before returning to her face. "That I can promise you."

The walk home was silent, surprising Gabby. Although she enjoyed quiet companionship, she knew that not many other people did. The twins met them at the door, bombarding Gabby with news of their day, informing her that they were going to eat outside, ushering them both through the house and out onto the patio. Gabby's father had lit several lanterns, a large picnic rug spread out beneath the peppercorn tree. Gabby's mother appeared in the doorway, holding a tray laden down with loaves of bread and fillings, Caleb rushing to take it from her, carrying it over to the rug as she instructed. Dinner was a perfect Italian feast, as it usually was in the Bianchi household. Lucia and Sofia were beside themselves, both having helped to prepare and plan the picnic. Gabby was happy to see chilled bottles of Chianti Classico amongst the rustic loaves of bread and antipasto platters, it wasn't often that she had the chance to enjoy a glass of wine, but when she did, Chianti Classico was her go-to drink of choice.

The meal passed too quickly, Gabby stretched out, her feet in front of her, and looked around their little group. They were transplants as her mother called them. Die-hard Italians who had emigrated to Australia in search of a better life for their children. They had settled in Queensland's capital, the premier city of Brisbane, and soon after had welcomed Gabby, and then a year later, her sister, Valentina. The girls had grown up in a mostly Italian neighbourhood, surrounded by noisy, Italian culture. Gabby had loved it, the sense of belonging, of community. Valentina had not. Her teenage years had been plagued by incidents of shoplifting and wagging school. In a last-ditch effort to steer their youngest away from bad influences, Maria and Nico had sold up and moved their family to Beryl Creek to start afresh. It had not been an easy adjustment, for any of them.

Maria and Nico had lost their large circle of friends, their community, and while they had adapted quickly and made new friends here, Nico and Maria remained the only Italian family in Beryl Creek. Valentina had thrived, commanding a large group of friends wherever she went, although she never did stop shoplifting, she just made sure that she and her friends travelled to a neighbouring town to do it, that was all. As for Gabby, she never really fit in. Studious, rather than social, she adjusted, but when it was time for her to go off to university, she wasn't especially heartbroken to leave Beryl Creek. She certainly never imagined that she would be voluntarily returning only a few short years later, that she would ever make this town her forever home. It was amazing, she thought, looking around the small gathering, just what it was that people would do for family.

Sofia and Lucia had brought out their portable CD player, had tuned the radio to a local pop station, excitedly gushing over each song in the top forty countdown. The squeals were deafening for the number one song, Shade, by The Three Odd Lizards. Gabby was pulled up onto the make-believe stage by Lucia and Sofia, for an impromptu performance, Gabby sometimes forgot how much fun it was to be silly.

"Do you want to tell me why oh oh oh oh oh oh ooooh," the three of the crooned into an invisible microphone. "You never looked at me, that way before, mm mm mm mm mm mmmm, and here I mmmm, seeing you a-gain, in a new-ew ew ew ew ew ew ew ew , shade!" As the song ended, the three giggling girls fell to the ground, a tangle of limbs and laughter, missing Caleb's pale face and guilty expression.

With the moon high in the sky, and Lucia and Sofia unable to hide their yawns any longer, Gabby declared it bedtime, seconded by Maria, who offered to read the girls a bedtime story. The girls knew that this meant at least another half an hour, that they could easily wheedle at least two stories from Maria, and happily said good night and followed her inside.

"I think I will turn in for the night as well," Nico spoke. "You two stay and finish the Chianti Classico," he suggested to Caleb and Gabby.

"Come on papa, I'll take you upstairs," Gabby stood, stretching.

"You'll come back though, right?" Nico urged. Gabby looked down at Caleb on the picnic rug, a predatory glint in his eyes. Every fibre in her being buzzed, he was nectar, and very, very dangerous. If she was sensible, she would stay inside, guard her heart and never see him again. And yet, there was something magnetic about the way she felt pulled towards him.

"Yes papa, I will come back downstairs."

Gabby had always loved this big old peppercorn tree, even as a child. It had been her secret retreat, a place to fume over her sister's antics, to cry over her mother's blatant favouritism and double standards, and to immerse herself in her latest novel.

"What is the difference between Chianti and Chianti Classico?" Caleb mused aloud. Gabby and Caleb had cleared the picnic rug, were now stretched out on their backs beneath the peppercorn tree, gazing up at the night sky, finishing the Chianti Classico, talking of everything and of nothing.

"The region in Italy where the grapes are grown," Gabby answered, remembering the time that she had asked her father the very same question. She had been treated to an hour-long lesson in Chianti, what made it so earthy and rustic, why it was high in tannins, the reason it dried your mouth out, how much acidity there was in the Chianti, why it tasted like strawberries and cherries, and the fact that is was so versatile that it went with not only classic Italian dishes but that it also worked perfectly well with pizza or grilled cheese.

"My parents took me there when I was fifteen, hopefully, one day I will be able to take the girls there for a holiday, they should see their heritage."

"Were you born in Italy?"

"No, Australia, but I'm proud to be an Italian Australia," Gabby smiled. "I get the best of both worlds."

"In what way?"

"Being Australian gives me the freedom to live in the best country in the world, to dress how I like, to say what I want without fear of appraisal. Being Italian," she smiled broadly, "is what gives me heart. Being Italian is more than just getting olive skin and a love of pasta. It means appreciating the little things, the colour of the sky, the curve of the mountain, the smell of the orange blossoms. It is experiencing the innocence of a child, and the loyalty of a dog. It is taking care of your family first, no matter what. It is making things by hand, for me, it is baking. It is being generous, stubborn, and proud of your heritage. Above all else, being Italian means people stick to their word. *La parole é sagral.*"

"What does that mean?"

"It means 'the word is blood', so don't ever cross us." She grinned.

CHAPTER SEVEN

"Why aren't you married?" Caleb blurted out, watching Gabby lazily.

"Excuse me?!" Gabby snorted indelicately. "What makes you think that I'm not married?"

"I just, I mean…" Caleb trailed off. "The girls never mention their dad, you don't either, I guess I just took that to mean that you were no longer married."

"I've never been married, oh, don't look so shocked."

"Not shocked, more like surprised. Your mum seems so traditional, I guess I just thought that you would be married when you had kids."

"There was a time I thought so too." A wistful sigh. "The girls aren't biologically mine, they are my sister's children."

"Oh, I'm sorry, they call you mum, I just figured…"

"Gosh, no, don't be sorry. I adopted them when they were only a few weeks old, I'm the only mum they have ever known."

"Wow, that's huge. What happened to your sister if you don't mind me asking?"

"Absolutely nothing happened to Valentina. She always had tickets on herself, she was never satisfied with anything she had. She worked our mother to the bone, always getting her to make her a fancy ball gown or buy her something that she just had to have," Gabby could no more keep the bitterness from her voice as she could have stopped the moon from shining.

"The last time Valentina was caught shoplifting, our parents moved us here, they hoped it would help her."

"But it didn't." Caleb surmised.

"No. The thing you need to understand about my sister is that she was always effervescent. People were drawn to her magnetism. She was always able to get what she wanted without lifting a finger. So, she found a new group of friends to hang out with and they were always in and out of trouble. By the time she was off to university, she had a large group of friends with benefits, or screw buddies as she called them. She made it very clear that if she were ever to fall pregnant, she would never tell anyone, she would simply have a termination and move on."

"What changed?"

"We live in a very small town," Gabby laughed. "Valentina came home for semester break, she purchased a pregnancy test from the pharmacy one town over, his wife is best friends with the lady who owns the newsagency here, and her brother plays cards with dad. So, yeah, they knew before she had walked back through the door. She had no way out; my parents are very conservative. The pregnancy had been the result of a consensual act, and therefore, was to be cherished. I was studying abroad; I received a call in the middle of the night telling me that I was needed at home. By the time Michael and I got back to town-"

"Woah, who's Michael?"

"Michael was my fiancé at the time," Gabby brushed his question aside. She was not going to think of Michael, especially not now, after all of this time. "When we got back to town, I was presented with two baby girls and adoption papers drawn up in my name only. Valentina graduated the following semester. She's a partner in a law firm now, last I heard she had cemented her position by marrying the boss's son." Gabby shrugged nonchalantly.

"She was always going to have an exit plan, of course, she never took responsibility for something if she could get someone else to do it for her. It was cunning really, if she was going to be made to do something she didn't want to do, then so was I." Gabby took a long sip from her glass. "She told our parents that she would place the girls for adoption, my parents begged her, pleaded with her to give the girls to them, but she refused. In the end, they struck up a deal. My parents agreed that I would adopt the girls, and in return, they would pay Valentina two hundred thousand dollars, which worked out to be her university fees and enough money to put a deposit on an inner-city apartment. That is what I returned home to."

"She sold her own children?" Caleb was dumbfounded, what sort of person would do that?

"They were never more than leverage to her."

"And you just went along with their deal?" It was obvious to Caleb that Gabby was a perfectionist, he wondered if she knew.

"What else could I have done Caleb? Refusing would have torn my family apart and driven the wedge even deeper between my parents and I." Gabby shook her head irritably, dislodging the hurt simmering just beneath the surface.

"You didn't get along with your parents? You seem so close now."

"Mm-hmm," Gabby was non-committal. "I guess it does seem that way, doesn't it? Not everything is as it seems, Caleb. Do I get along with them? On some level, yes. There is also a lot of resentment there. I would like to say that it is fading over time, but the truth is, it is only now becoming apparent to me.

My parents bent over backwards to cater to my sister and her whims, at the expense of me. It was always simply expected that I would go along with whatever was required, and I did, to keep the peace. The adoption was the final straw. To not be consulted or even asked, that stung." She remembered the shock of walking in the house, of seeing the two girls sleeping in her father's arms, of discovering that her sister had been pregnant, of hearing what her parents had agreed to do on her behalf, the anger that had followed her around like a fog for weeks afterwards.

"It was not what Michael had signed up for, the fact that I was Italian was more than enough for his wealthy family to have to cope with as it was."

"He broke off the engagement?" Caleb surmised.

"It was just as well," Gabby nodded, "I found out later that he had been having an affair with someone I considered a friend, one of my fellow students in Paris."

"What were you studying?"

"What? Oh, I was training to become a pastry chef in Paris."

"Hence the bakery?"

"Actually no," Gabby smiled fondly, "my parents always had the bakery, although it used to do much better. Paying off Valentina nearly bankrupted my parents. When I returned home and found the twins waiting for me, I had no other option, of course, I withdrew from my studies in Paris. I started working full time in the bakery, I used to take the girls in with me, we had a portable cot set up in one corner of the kitchen. That all stopped just shy of their first birthday."

"Ah, that must have been when you decided to take a break and do something nice for yourself." Caleb joked, not imagining for one moment that Gabby would ever voluntarily take a break from the bakery. He tried to picture two little cherubs in a portable cot, gosh she must have been run off her feet. He wondered if her mother had helped in the bakery at all, from what he could tell, she seemed to potter around the house most of the day. Semi-retired maybe?

"Ha!" Gabby snorted indelicately. "As if!" Gabby knew there were those that thought her weak for putting herself last, but it was her choice…mostly. She knew it stemmed from never doing anything right in the eyes of her mother. For better or for worse, family is first and foremost the most important thing in her life, she is the gel that keeps in contact with all of her extended family, if she didn't make the time, the effort, then who would? It is why family holidays and birthdays are such a huge part of her life, the reason why she never allows a birthday to go past without a celebration, why she stays up until the wee hours of the morning, just to make sure that there is a special cake and dinner for the person celebrating a birthday. It was doing all the little things that reminded her of sitting in her grandmother's lap while she fed her bites of her toast dipped in coffee. Gabby would savour the buttery, coffee flavours and the secondary crunch of toast, surrounded by feelings of warmth and love. To this day, that was still the best toast she had ever tasted.

"It was a horrid time for us. My mother and I were always arguing, about big things, who was actually raising the girls and how, and about the little things like rebranding the bakery, and what to cook for dinner. Honestly," Gabby shook her head sadly, "it really was just an awful time. Right in the middle of one of our arguments, dad keeled over. He spent months in the hospital in Sydney, recovering from a severe stroke. It is why he is in a wheelchair."

"Gabby, I don't know what to say, that's awful!" Caleb reached for Gabby's hand instinctively, entwining his fingers with hers, a warmth spreading through him when she didn't resist or pull away. "Will he ever fully recover?"

"The doctors aren't sure; it is quite simply a waiting game."

"It must be so hard for him, for all of you."

"It has been especially hard for mum, she is unable to help out much, physically at least, and dad is easily frustrated by his limitations. Mostly, I think he is embarrassed at not being able to provide for his family, at having to depend on me for the simple act of getting up and down the stairs." She sighed deeply.

"You carry him up and down the stairs?!"

"It's more like a piggyback really," she chuckled, "seriously, he doesn't weigh very much, and we don't have the money to install a stairlift, so…" she shrugged. "It is what it is."

"That's a lot on your plate Gabby, isn't there anyone else who can help out?" Caleb felt uneasy, it wasn't often that he thought about money, or anything really. If he wanted something, he merely had to voice his desire and it was delivered to him without him ever needing to lift a finger. He was starting to see how entitled that must look to others, a realisation that did not sit well with Caleb.

"Half the town would help, and they do in their own ways, but my mother is a very private person, she would rather struggle in silence than let anyone know how she was really doing. Sometimes I worry that she will never recover, emotionally, I mean. If we lose the bakery, well…Who knows."

"It sounds like you need a miracle," Caleb mused aloud.

"Or maybe just a little magic from great great great grandmother Beryl." Gabby grinned.

Laughter drifted up on the breeze, bringing a smile to Nico's face. It had been so long, too long, since he had heard Gabby laugh like that. It made his heart happy, not that his wife, Maria, would see it that way. With a deep sigh, he tugged the rope that would pull his window closed, cutting off the sound, once again plunging his bedroom into endless silence as thick as sludge. He wished there was a way to get through to Maria, he wished she weren't so harsh with Gabby. If only the harshness came out of a place of worry or concern, but Nico was forced to admit that it did not. Maria had always been this way with Gabby, but things had become a lot worse after Valentina was born. Their youngest daughter had always been very…Nico gave himself a mental shake. No, he would not make excuses for her. Valentina was selfish, that was what she was, and she always had been. Nothing was ever good enough for her, no matter how much of a strain it had put on Nico or Maria. It was a price Nico and Maria paid willingly, as parents always did, but it had been Gabby who had suffered the most, always playing second fiddle to her younger sibling, always biting her tongue lest she upset her unwillingly, so unstable was Valentina's emotions.

The eldest, Gabby was as different from Valentina as night was from day. As first-time parents, Nico and Maria used to joke that Gabby had been born an old soul, a trait that soon became a hindrance. Gabby was always the good girl, the one to toe the line and never make any trouble. When Nico and Maria missed her school performances because Valentina insisted they both attend her weekly swimming lessons, Gabby didn't object. Nico knew that he and Maria had taken advantage of that. Oh, they hadn't wanted to, it was just easier, knowing that Gabby would happily accommodate whatever

Valentina needed, happily and without any fuss. He regretted it now, not doing more to help her find her voice. Maybe if he had, Maria and Gabby would have a more amicable relationship, instead of the often strained one that they currently had. Nico adored his wife, Maria had been his first love and he knew she would be his only love, but there were times when he had turned a blind eye when he should have spoken out.

He knew Maria loved Gabby as unconditionally as he did, but there were times that Nico knew Valentina had been her favourite, there were times when Gabby knew it too. The curse of being an old man stuck inside a wheelchair was that it gave Nico way too much time to simply think and to reflect on all of his past mistakes, and there were days when the numbers were simply too great to bear. He knew that he and Maria had failed Gabby, that night when Valentina came to them pregnant and gloating, the benefit of hindsight. He sighed deeply. He wished he could go back, undo all of the things he had gotten wrong. If only there was a way to make everything right, to give Gabby the life she deserved, to get her away from this small town, to give her the opportunities that she missed out on. He wished that he could get Maria on board, wished there was a way to soften her reserve when it came to Gabby. He knew she hated being so harsh with her, he knew she wanted to be involved in her life, he also knew that she just didn't know how.

For now though, Gabby was happy, that was all that Nico could ask for. Tomorrow, well, tomorrow would have to take care of itself.

CHAPTER EIGHT

Laughing, Caleb turned to look at Sam, his eyes twinkling. "See," he couldn't help teasing the other man, "I knew you would have a good time tonight Sammy."

"I always have a good time with you little brother," Sam ruffled Caleb's perfectly lacquered hair, deliberately squashing the rock star 'ruffled fresh from bed' style that Caleb had spent hours perfecting earlier that night. "But we can't all be irresponsible rockstars now can we, Callie?" Sam used the childhood nickname he knew Caleb detested so much, knowing it would get a rise out of him. "Some of us actually have to work to earn a living!" It was the same banter that always existed between them, the ribbing and poking fun that was laced with the love that comes from being part of a family.

"Work?!" snorted Caleb, "Ha! As if! You're a partner in a law firm Sammy, how much work can you possibly do? Don't you have a staff of people all waiting to jump to your command?" Caleb's raucous laugh mingled with Sam's deep chortle.

"Staff? That's your department brother dear, how many do you have now? Eighteen? Ninete-"

"Watch out!" Caleb's panicked shout interrupts Sam, and he blinks once, surprise etching his features. The unrelenting screech of bare metal tyre rims on bitumen reaches a crescendo before fading into silence, the world turning black.

Caleb moaned softly, pain radiating from his shoulder. He squeezed his eyes shut tight, then opened them, blinking rapidly until the stars overhead came into focus. He turned his head slightly, eyes searching in the half-light for Sam. Where was he? With momentous effort, Caleb hauled himself into an upright position, ignoring the trickle of blood running down his face, waving away the concerned faces hovering in front of him. He looked around, why was everyone moving so slowly? Where was Gabby?

"Mum?" Why was his mum here, had she come to the wedding? Standing at the edge of the road, watching him, smiling in expectation, were his parents. His dad waved at him. What were they doing here? Where was Sam?

Caleb turned towards the small crowd that had gathered in the middle of the road, a short distance from the chapel. Everyone was out of focus, nothing made sense. Did someone drug him at the reception? Sam should be here. He looked down, his hands were covered in blood, so much blood. He blinked, looked down at the road, saw Sam's sneakers sticking out from the crowd gathered. Funny, Caleb didn't remember moving. The crowd parted, Sam laid on the road, hands linked behind his head, a boyish smile etched onto his face.

"Sam, what are you doing, this is a road, you can't stay here, we'll be late."

"Look at the stars little brother," Sam flicked his hand in the direction of the night sky. "You're a star, you know that right? You're translucendal Cal, translucendal." Sam drew the last word out, slowly enunciating every single syllable.

"What are you talking about," Caleb's voice sounded so far away, even to his own ears. "That not even a word Sam, you just made it up."

"I'm pretty sure it's a word little brother, and if not, it should be." Sam smiled up at Caleb. "It's what you are, Caleb, don't forget that. Translucendal."

"Sam, enough," Caleb frowned, consternation etching his features. "Why are you lying here? What are we doing, come on, we need to go."

"Cal." Sam only called him that when he was being serious, which was a rare thing. "We are already here."

"What are you talking about, you're not making any sense."

"Don't you remember Cal? You killed me. I died a slow and painful death, that's why you are all alone now, everyone left you, Cal, everyone". Caleb looked up, he was surrounded by ghostly images, vague memories of people he once knew, nothing solid to hang on to.

Caleb sat bolt upright, sweat dripping from his brow. Darn it, he thought he had already endured the worst of the nightmares, thought he had reached the point where he had them under control, where they no longer plagued him night after night, where they had become more infrequent. Obviously, he was wrong. As much as Caleb wished he could feign ignorance, he couldn't, he knew why the nightmares had amplified in the last few weeks. It was almost a year since Sam had gone, twelve months of waiting for him to walk back through the door, of scanning faces in the crowd, hoping to see his trademark grin. Caleb knew that he would have to face it head-on, at some point he was going to have to take responsibility for his actions, would have to eventually go to his parents and seek their forgiveness. He just wasn't ready yet, he needed more time, was that too much to ask for? He honestly didn't know.

When Caleb downstairs for breakfast he was surprised to see Gabby at the table with Lucia and Sofia.

"Good morning ladies," he announced his presence, winking at Gabby and earning giggles from Lucia and Sofia. "No work today?" He asked Gabby, helping himself to a coffee scroll.

"On Friday I open the bakery up a little later." Gabby smiled at Caleb over her mug of steaming coffee. "We stay open later to compensate, on Friday nights there is a street market of sorts here in Beryl Creek, all the stores stay open later, some of the local farmers bring in their produce, there are usually stalls run by local kids selling lemonade, there are craft stalls and cake stalls and the vet will have a stall for people to adopt stray animals," Gabby fixed Lucia and Sofia with a hard stare, "which we will not be taking advantage of. Anyway, it is always fun, the local Lions Club will do a barbeque and the money raised goes to a different charity each week. Tonight, the money goes to the local school, they are trying to fund the purchase of some new musical instruments. You should come with us tonight; it will be fun."

"Does everyone in town go?" Caleb had to admit, it did sound like fun, but he was hesitant to commit to going, he didn't want to impose on Gabby and her family, especially after yesterday at the bakery.

"The whole town," Lucia replied around a mouthful of pancake, stretching her hands wide to emphasise her point.

"Goodness, that sounds like a fun market to go to."

"Yup, it is. Plus," she added thoughtfully, "they have balloons you can buy if you've been good." Gabby and Caleb exchanged a sideways glance, it was obvious that Lucia was hoping that she had been good enough to be able to get a balloon tonight.

"Okay then, I would love to come with you ladies, if you'll let me accompany you?"

"If you want to come with mum and dad and the girls, we'll meet at the bakery a little after five o'clock this afternoon." Gabby downed the last of her coffee, rising from the table and kissing the girls.

"What happens to the bakery?" Caleb remembered that Gabby had said that she kept it open late for the crowds.

"Mum and I will take it in turns to work in the bakery and head out into the market with Lucia and Sofia." Gabby paused in the doorway. "Dad will help out too if he feels up to it. So, I will see you all later, have a good day." Gabby tried not to sound too excited at the prospect of spending more time with Caleb, after all, he was a guest, that was all. She wasn't a teenager with a silly little crush for goodness sake, she was a grown woman with twin daughters, she was not going to lose her head, or her heart, she was more sensible than that, wasn't she? As long as he didn't kiss her again or look at her for that matter. If that happened, well, she had no chance of keeping her self control, she knew that for sure. If the kiss at the bakery yesterday was anything to go by, she would be completely lost.

Gabby found herself humming to herself as she went about baking and prepping the bakery for the day. There was a lightness about her today, something that she had not felt for so long, perhaps ever. She whipped up her usual loaves of bread and pastries, biscuits and pies, cakes and tarts, and then having an hour to spare until opening, she made a special batch of novelty shaped meringues, knowing just how much Sofia and Lucia loved them. The day was busy, as well as her usual customers, there was the added foot traffic of the tourists in town for the weekend's camel races. Being busy certainly made the day go faster, and it wasn't long before Lucia and Sofia were bounding through the door, excitedly exclaiming over all of the treasures that they had already seen, and which they absolutely had to show her. Gabby laughed and allowed herself to be led out of the bakery by little hands eagerly clutching hers, Caleb following behind, her mum and dad assuring her that they would hold down the fort at the bakery and that there was no reason for her to hurry back.

The four of them all but ran down to the end of the main street, Lucia and Sofia determined that they needed to start the market at the very beginning. Gabby tended to agree, she and the girls hated to miss out on any aspect of the local markets. As she had predicted, Lucia and Sofia led them straight to the local vet's stall with all the cutest of puppies and kittens in desperate need of a forever home.

"Look mama, isn't it adorable?!" Lucia gently picked up a tiny kitten, cradling it close to her chest.

"Yes, Lucia, it is very cute," Gabby agreed, watching her daughter snuggle with the kitten. She had to admit, it was a sweet thing, a ginger longhair. Gabby sighed and touched her daughter's shoulder. "Come on Lucia, pop him back now, there are other people wanting to look at the animals too." Gabby didn't miss the crestfallen expression on her daughter's face, she knew how much Lucia wished there was a cat in the house.

"Don't be sad Lucia, you can always cuddle Bella," Sofia took her sister's hand, trying to comfort her.

"Bella is your dog, not mine," Lucia answered sullenly. "Nanna got her for you, not me."

"I don't mind sharing her, besides, she loves cuddles." Sofia thought this made perfect sense. It concerned Gabby, the fact that Lucia believed that her nanna had purchased a pet for her sister, but not for her. The girls wandered off ahead, Gabby and Caleb following more slowly behind.

"Is what she said true?" Caleb asked Gabby softly. "Did Maria really buy Sofia Bella?"

"It was correct enough, but the reasoning behind it was not as clear cut as Lucia thought they were. There was a time when Sofia was incredibly anxious, she would barely leave the house, she suffered from horrid nightmares. Bella was suggested by her therapist, and she has helped enormously."

"So now Lucia is feeling a little lonely?" Caleb guessed.

"Yes. She was too young to understand why Sofia got Bella, she only understood that her sister got a dog and she didn't. Suddenly, instead of going and doing everything with her twin, she was left out of the loop, it was Sofia and Bella going everywhere and doing everything together. Mum didn't mean for Lucia to feel left out, it was just that at the time, mum did was she thought was best."

"Would it be completely impossible for Lucia to get that kitten?"

"Caleb," there was a warning in Gabby's voice. "Do you know who would end up looking after the kitten? The same person who looks after Bella. Me." Gabby shot Caleb a sideways glance. "It wouldn't be impossible," Gabby sighed. "Okay, I'll go and see how much they are wanting for the little fluffball."

"Let me go," Caleb surprised himself by offering.

"Okay, just remember to haggle. Oh, and Caleb," Gabby turned back to Caleb. "I don't want to have to spend more than fifty dollars."

Caleb didn't know how much kittens, or any type of animal for that matter, cost, but he was surprised to think it would be as much as fifty dollars. He jogged back to the vet stall, waiting patiently while the lady ahead of him discussed the pros and cons of possibly adopting a great dane. When she was finally finished, Caleb pounced on the vet.

"The ginger kitten there, how much are you hoping to get for it?"

"It is open to offers sir, all the animals are. We want them to go to good homes, so we ask that you only pay what you can afford. We would rather the animals have food, toys and a bed, if you spent too much on the adoption, they wouldn't get the best you can give them, would they?"

"Where does the money you raise from the sale of these animals go?"

"All proceeds go to funding our shelter, we are a no-kill shelter, and costs do add up."

"I will give you one thousand dollars for the orange fluff ball."

When Caleb caught up with Gabby, Sofia and Lucia, he had a huge grin on his face, and a furry orange fluff ball sticking out of his coat pocket.

"Hey, mister Roman, it is that kitten I saw," Lucia spotted it right away, her voice wistful.

"It is. Actually, Lucia, I asked your mum if it would be okay, and she said it would be, so I went back and bought him, for you. I would like you to have him, as a gift." Her unexpected shrieks caused more than a few people nearby to jump in alarm, Gabby hurrying to shush her young daughter. Lucia all but swooped the kitten out of Caleb's hands, holding him to her face and smothering him with soft kisses.

"Lucia, what are you going to name him?" Gabby nudged.

"Jellybean", Lucia didn't hesitate with her answer, making Gabby wonder just how long she had been wishing and hoping for a pet of her own.

With Jellybean firmly in her grip, Lucia was content to simply follow Sofia as she pointed out all of her finds to Gabby, not interested in anything now that she had Jellybean. Gabby and Caleb made it a point to check in on Lucia and Jellybean frequently, but she proudly declared that they were fine together and that she could take care of him all by herself. Gabby purchased herself some fresh produce from a local farmer's stall, and a couple of books for her father from the local primary school stall, Caleb finding a stack of old vinyl records and paying the local hospital ladies auxiliary a staggering amount of money by way of a donation to their fund. Gabby thought it was an exorbitant amount to donate, the way he winked at her when she softly chided him about it turned her insides to mush and caused a light blush to flood her cheeks. Her only blessing was the falling darkness, although she was pretty sure that Caleb had seen it, by the way his wink turned into a full-throated laugh.

They stopped for burgers with the lot, the size of dinner plates, with hot chips on the side, carrying their bags back to the bakery and spreading their feast out on the kitchen table with Maria and Nico. They left the bakery open, Gabby was happy to pop in and out of the kitchen to serve customers while they ate their feast. Lucia barely touched her burger, too enamoured with her kitten, both her nanna and her poppy having inspected him, declaring him a fine kitten, with a fun name. Sofia had no such issues, happily chowing into her burger, she was like her mama, when she asked for the lot, she meant the lot. There was bacon, egg, beetroot, pineapple, lettuce, tomato, steak, cheese, and cucumber oozing out the sides, with a generous amount of tomato sauce smeared across her face. Luckily Gabby wasn't nearly as messy. They closed the bakery up shortly before ten o'clock, the noisy group walking back home together, bags of purchases distributed evenly except for Jellybean, still tucked tightly in Lucia's arms. As everyone said goodnight and made their way to bed, Gabby smiled at how nice the evening had been.

Laughing, Caleb turned to look at Sam, his eyes twinkling. "See," he couldn't help teasing the other man, "I knew you would have a good time tonight Sammy."

"I always have a good time with you little brother," Sam ruffled Caleb's perfectly lacquered hair, deliberately squashing the rock star 'ruffled fresh from bed' style that Caleb had spent hours perfecting earlier that night. "But we can't all be irresponsible rockstars now can we, Callie?" Sam used the childhood nickname he knew Caleb detested so much, knowing it would get a rise out of him. "Some of us actually have to work to earn a living!" It was the same banter that always existed between them, the ribbing and poking fun that was laced with the love that comes from being part of a family.

"Work?!" snorted Caleb, "Ha! As if! You're a partner in a law firm Sammy, how much work can you possibly do? Don't you have a staff of people all waiting to jump to your command?" Caleb's raucous laugh mingled with Sam's deep chortle.

"Staff? That's your department brother dear, how many do you have now? Eighteen? Ninete-"

"Watch out!" Caleb's panicked shout interrupts Sam, and he blinks once, surprise etching his features. The unrelenting screech of bare metal tyre rims on bitumen reaches a crescendo before fading into silence, the world turning black, the only sound an incessant beep, beep, beep.

Breakfast was a noisy affair, Caleb, unable to fall back to sleep after his nightmare, already had the makings of a headache. Sofia and Lucia were fairly dancing in their chairs, as they excitedly told him, today was day one of the local camel cup. As endearing as they both were, Caleb thought they were way too excited over the prospect of watching a bunch of camels racing around a track, although he would never have told them so. To be honest, he had never actually seen a camel race, but the thought of it was beyond him. What on earth was so appealing about seeing camels running around a racetrack? Then again, Caleb had never been overly interested in racing in any form. He just simply did not see the point. Despite his reservations, he could feel a sense of curiosity starting to churn in his stomach, no doubt a side effect of being exposed to Sofia and Lucia. It promised to be an interesting day, and then, of course, there was Gabby…

Trouble, that was what she was, he decided as he helped to pack up the cars in order to leave. Logically, he knew that she was trouble, he really did, it was just that, she made him smile. Which, he guessed, was the real reason why he needed to stay well away from her. In the past twelve months, he could count on one hand the number of times that he had smiled, and all of them had happened in the last few days that he had been staying in Beryl Creek. Not that he intended to examine that, at least not now, maybe not ever. Even if he wasn't irreparably broken inside, he had nothing to offer in the relationship stakes anymore. Sure, he had the money and fame and all the things that came with that status, but deep down, they were empty gestures. He sucked as a boyfriend, always lost in his own head, in his music, never remembering to return calls, forgetting birthdays and special dates, heck, he rarely remember to eat most days! No, certainly nothing to offer, and, he reminded himself, he had no time for entanglements, not now, and certainly not with a woman who already had enough on her plate. No, Gabby deserved a lot more than he was willing to offer right now.

"Caleb, are you listening to me?" Gabby stood before him, hand on hip, sunglasses flipped to the top of her head, waiting.

"I'm sorry, I was miles away." Liar, his inner voice taunted him, you were too busy watching the way she moved in her dress.

"I was saying that the Beryl Creek Camel Cup race is one of the more unique events on the outback calendar," Gabby explains as they start loading up the car with what she called essentials. Seriously, if his band carried this many essentials, they would need a Hercules aircraft to tour with them. Aside from the six folding chairs, there were three Esky's full of food and drinks, a folding table, two picnic blankets, the obligatory camera, assorted books and toys both Lucia and Sofia insisted that they could not live without, sweaters in case the weather gets cooler, and a box of medical supplies. Caleb raised his eyes at the last item, they were going as spectators after all, not competitors. "It is all hands on deck Caleb, when someone gets hurt." Caleb found the use of 'when' not 'if' a touch concerning, but Gabby just continued. "Camels are completely unpredictable, as are the crazies who decide to ride them in the races, so…" She trailed off.

"What do you mean, the crazies who decide to ride them? Don't they have, you know, actual riders, like with horses?"

"You mean jockeys?" Gabby can't resist teasing him. "And no, not for the camel races. Anyone from the crowd can sign on to ride a camel in a race, as long as they sign a waiver stating that they won't hold the Beryl Creek Council liable if they are injured, or, you know," she shrugged, "die as a result."

"Are you kidding me right now?!"

"No."

"So, you're serious? Anyone can just put their hand up and jump on a camel?"

"Sure, if they are reckless enough and have no fear of…Wait. Caleb, you're not thinking about putting your hand up, are you?" A frown creased her brow, cute as it was, Caleb brushed her concern aside.

"Goodness no, I was just wondering." Gabby fixed him with a hard stare that Caleb tried hard not to fidget under. She was inscrutable, she would have given his mother a run for her money in that area, of this he was sure. Deciding that he was, in fact, telling her the truth, or maybe just wanting to let him off the hook, she nodded once, and moved to finish cramming the gear into the back of her ancient station wagon. She had nothing to worry about, even if he was in his rock star persona, he would never have risked such a stunt. He was far too much of a coward, besides, he was flying under the radar here.

"Good, the last thing we need is two strong-willed invalids to care for," she snaps at him. "So, you'll meet some of the nicest people at the cup today. Good people, honest people. Of course, there will be just as many crackpots, which is part of the fun." She smiled at him.

"The crackpots?"

"No, telling them apart." She laughed. "You'll see, it will be fun." The more that Caleb heard about the camel races, the more intrigued he became. He was not, however, in any way prepared for the sight that greeted him upon their arrival at Williamsfield Park. Streams of golden light dance across the mountains surrounding the park, ring-necked parrots dance and sway beneath the clouds. Children run past waving ribbons behind them, a couple kisses as if no one is watching. Gabby had told him on the ride over that there would be a field of twenty camels taking part in the races this weekend, with eight race heats all culminating in tomorrow's semi and grand finales. More than just a camel race, it was also a carnival. It was hard to believe that he was only five kilometres from the centre of town, from Gabby's bakery, this park felt like he had entered another world.

The crowd was a melting pot brimming with locals, tourists and families; there were men in chequered shirts and battered Akubras, and canny locals combining fashion and comfort by affixing fascinators to woollen beanies, despite the fact that it was nowhere near freezing at twenty-something degrees. He was glad they arrived as early as they did, the fields used for parking was already six rows deep, full of utes, campervans, and trailers, with more lining the road trying to get in. There are rows and rows of food vendors, each selling a single cuisine, their lines already long despite the early hour. There were hotdogs, strawberries and cream, corn on the cob, baked potatoes. He could already hear Sofia and Lucia petitioning their Poppy for something called a potato twist, whatever that was. The unease grew in his stomach, people were always amazed whenever he admitted that he was shy. He, a world-famous guitarist. People thought he was being cute with them, that he simply didn't want to talk. It crippled him at times, his shyness, it had become a braking mechanism of sorts for him, at times drenching his day in anxiety.

They found a spot to set up their chairs and blankets, under the shade of an ancient grove of trees, close enough to the car for trips back to get the food, and flat enough for Nico to manoeuvre his wheelchair comfortably. The view of the track is close enough to catch all of the action, but far enough back to ease Maria's fear of injury by crazy camels. At the end of the field a judge's box stands on stilts, the judging job far from strenuous, it is usually clear which camel comes first, these races are rarely marked by a photo finish. Unlike horse racing, which is a glamourous affair, camel racing is anything but. Horses behave like gentlemen, camels are bawdy. They spit. They stomp. They kick. They do whatever it is that takes their fancy, heck, some even refuse to run.

CHAPTER NINE

The races start with a mini-history lesson, re-enacted for the families and tourists in attendance. The speaker was good, Caleb had to admit, even he was mesmerized. They spoke of camels having hailed from Afghanistan, Arabia and India, of coming to Australia to provide a transport system that was not dependent on water, of their aid in the exploration and establishment of communications routes, especially throughout the outback. Once trains arrived, camels were redundant and were simply set free into the wild, despite the environmental headache. Caleb thought that wild was an accurate way to describe their nature, he and Gabby having taken Lucia and Sofia to the camel holding pens before the races so that the girls could choose their favourites to back. The camels showed off their very best grunts, spitting and making horrid groaning sounds as they walked around making their choices. Despite this, the girls both chose their favourites, declaring that Tim Tam Jam and Mr Pickles were both handsome specimens who would surely win. Caleb thought they were all crazy.

The day finally kicked off with possibly the worst rendition of the national anthem that Caleb has ever heard. He looks around, if the pained expressions on everyone else's faces are anything to go by, he is not the only one to feel this way. Three long minutes he sits there, trying to compose a neutral expression on his face. For three long minutes, he knows, he counted the seconds in his head, a group of amateur singers transport the crowd's collective eardrums to hell. Awkward silence and weak clapping ensue, the singers not at all fazed, one going as far as leaning into the microphone and whispering an apology. Sunglasses on, Caleb leans back in his folding chair, happy just to crowd watch. Nico regales Sofia and Lucia with stories from the early camel cup days. Rumour has it, in the late sixties, two friends decided to settle an argument by pitting their camels against each other in a race along the Beryl Creek. The crazy race has run every year since, although they have had several upgrades since then. As well as the camel races, the carnival includes belly dancing, kids' rides, an animal farm, fashions on the field, wood carving demonstrations using a chainsaw, and numerous other events all aimed at showcasing the local community.

"Gabby, look," Nico shot Caleb a surreptitious wink. "fashions in the field is about to start, you should go sign up."

"Are you out of your mind?" Gabby baulked at the suggestion. "You want me to enter a fashion parade?"

"You are a beautiful woman Gabby, you will win for sure, no?" Nico chuckled. "You are just like your mama sometimes."

"Huh," Maria snorts from her vantage spot on Nico's left. "I raise my Gabby to have taste and class Nico, not to parade around on display for men to ogle her."

"What's ogle mean?" Piped up Lucia.

"Great, thank you guys," Gabby hissed to her parents. "Ogle means to look at sweetheart," she explained to Lucia.

"Why don't you want men to look at you? You're a very pretty mummy, don't you want to get a husband?" Caleb thought he would literally choke on his coffee, Nico leaned over and slapped him hard on the back.

"That is not how you get a husband Lucia, where do you girls hear about such things?"

"Poppy let us watch Strut It with him."

"He what!?" Caleb wondered if steam would shoot from Gabby's ears. "Dad, that was-"

"Nico, how could you?" Maria interrupted Gabby, both women now shooting angry looks at Nico, caught in the headlights of their gazes.

"It was only a little bit of fun."

"I'm not talking about the stupid television show Nico, I am talking about Sofia and Lucia. They don't need a father any more than Gabby needs a husband."

"Seriously guys, you know we are all sitting right here, right?" Gabby warns in an undertone. "Enough, both of you! Firstly, if I ever decide to marry, it will be to someone who thinks more of me than just my looks. Secondly, why wouldn't I want to marry someday mum? Just because I haven't yet, doesn't mean I never will. In any case, it is not up for discussion, do you understand?" She stands and brushes off some invisible dirt from her sundress. "Lucia, Sofia, come on, the line for the potato twist is not that long, let's go get some".

A glance at Nico and Maria and Caleb jumped up, quickly joining the girls in their hunt for food. "Well, that was...interesting," Caleb shoved his hands in his pockets, not trusting himself to take Gabby's hand otherwise. "Just so you know, it wouldn't have been a fair competition, you would have won hands down," he grinned at her, earning a smile in return.

"Shut up," Gabby mutters, looping her arm through his. They continue on in silence, a good thing, considering that Gabby had rendered Caleb speechless. Food ordered and paid for, potato twists for the girls and Nico, strawberries and cream for Maria, hot cinnamon doughnuts for Gabby, and one of literally everything he saw for Caleb, they headed back to their seats, eager to watch the unfolding parade.

"Are you sure you bought enough food, Caleb?" Nico jested as the food was passed around.

"Leave him alone, he's a growing lad," Maria defended, leaving the group in stitches.

The fashions on the field started innocently enough but soon turned into chaos when one of the contestants 'accidentally' tripped another, who, unfortunately, landed in a pile of camel dung from yesterday's practice round. In the end, the judges crowned a miss Jenna Barnes from Queensland as the winner, further proof that the camel cup has become more than just a local event, that it attracts tourists from all over the country. Jenna came to Beryl Creek on the spur of the moment, her young family keen for a weekend getaway. When accepting her award, a gold trophy in the shape of a camel, Jenna confessed that she had entered as a joke, wearing her mother's outfit, a floral pantsuit, that was last seen aboard a cruise ship well before Jenna was even born. Caleb had never laughed so hard in his life. Heck, this was a hoot! He could well imagine himself coming back here, to the camel races, he might even try and convince his band to do a community gig here, they would get a kick out of that. As famous as they all were now, they all enjoyed a simple life, coming from nothing, they enjoyed giving back when they could, and events like this, fun and weird, was right up their alley. His laugh died on his lips. If he brought them here, he would have to tell Gabby who he was, and that was something that could never happen.

At midday, six camels enter the field, ready to run in the first heat. Caleb watches, fascinated, as the call is put out to the audience, looking for spectators game enough to come forward and ride. He can sense Gabby watching him from the corner of her eye, was she really that concerned that he would put his hand up? He was flattered that she cared enough if he was being honest. As people started to come forward, either in bravery or stupidity, Caleb wasn't sure, a flock of galahs squawk in support. The starting line is bedlam as riders and trainers alike attempt to get the camels into a seated position, which, traditionally, is how they start a race. It did not go well. There were camels everywhere, an exotic looking woman calls to the closest camel rider to put their foot down. Caleb has no idea what she is talking about, and sadly it seems neither did the rider. The starting pistol is fired, camels are away, gangly legs wobbling all over the place. Dust covers the track and those who made the mistake of sitting too close. There are camels going in all directions, at top speed, as riders cling on for dear life. This is the craziest race Caleb has ever seen, and for a split second, he wished Sam was here with him, he would have loved this.

Gabby stands up and wanders through the throng of visitors lounging on blankets and chairs, over to the exotic looking woman Caleb saw talking to the camel riders before. "Hi, I'm Gabby, we own the bakery in town." She smiles down at the woman.
"I'm Sascha Fazulla, it's nice to meet you, you make the nicest Tiramisu I have ever tried. Would you like to join me?"
"I'd love to," Gabby sits cross-legged on the blanket next to Sascha. "I heard you calling out to the racers before, how

did you know what they needed to do, are you a camel trainer?"

"My ancestors are some of the Afghan cameleers who came to Australia many years ago, they settled in Broken Hill and the Oodnadatta area. I actually rode a camel to my wedding, and now my husband and I own a camel farm, we have always kept that strong camel connection".

"That sounds so exciting," Gabby was more than a little wistful, she had never had a proper adventure, if she was being honest with herself, she was a tad envious. "Camels are beautiful creatures, their rolling, swaying gait is so unusual, like a dance," Sascha says, "it is why they are referred to as ships in the desert. I simply love camels, I cannot imagine my life without them, they are full of character, or personality, plus, I like surprising people." As much as Gabby wanted to stay and talk, she could see her girls getting weary. She excused herself, exchanging contact details with Sascha and arranging to meet up at the finales tomorrow, before heading back to her own spot with her family. Heats pass, the eskies are emptied, much to Caleb's surprise, he honestly did not think that they would manage to eat their way through the mountains of food Maria had insisted on bringing with them, perhaps it was all of the fresh air and excitement that made them so hungry?

As the sun started to set, it was a tired group that made their way back to the cars, Nico and Maria holding fast to Sofia and Lucia while Gabby and Caleb carried their assorted gear. Nico insisted on overseeing Caleb as he loaded the cars back up, Maria and Gabby indulged him, helping get Lucia and Sofia in their seats, chatting about dinner plans, the girls trying to convince Maria and Gabby that ice cream and hot dogs would be the best idea. Caleb wasn't sure they would win that argument, the sound of their chatter bringing a smile to his face.

"You should take her out to dinner," Nico spoke softly.

"Gabby?" Caleb frowned, not sure if he had understood Nico correctly.

"Yes Gabby, unless there is something going on between you and my wife that I should know about," Nico joked, earning a chuckle from Caleb.

"No sir."

"Good. Then take Gabby to dinner. Tonight. We'll watch the girls." He clapped Caleb on the shoulder as he wheeled past. "Maria let's go. Caleb will ride back with Gabby."

Caleb and Gabby waved the car off until it exited the carpark and turned the corner. Making a move towards the car, Caleb took his chance and caught Gabby's hand in his.

"Have dinner with me?" He sounded breathless, his heart pounded, he thought he might be about to have a heart attack, which would be pretty ironic.

"Dinner? With you?" She looked at him curiously.

"Yes with me, I just thought…" Caleb trailed off. Oh God, if she didn't want to, Caleb wasn't sure what he would do.

"When?"

"Right now, tonight. Your dad said your parents will watch the kids tonight," Caleb pulled her closer, tilting her head upwards until her eyes met his. "So, will you have dinner with me Gabby?" She met his gaze head-on, questioning, probing.

"Yes," her voice husky, a slow smile curved her lips, "I will." His head closed the distance between their faces slowly, wanting to give her time to pull away if she wanted to, praying that she wouldn't. Their lips met, softly, a hope, a promise. His hands slid around her back, angled her closer to him as he deepened the kiss, uncaring of the people walking past.

Caleb broke off their kiss reluctantly, and steered Gabby to the front passenger door, opening it and helping her inside the car.

Caleb tried not to look too smug as he slid into the driver seat, accepting the keys from Gabby, and bringing the engine to life.

"So," Gabby started as he pulled out into the traffic. "Where are we going?"

"Bradford," Caleb answered with more confidence than he felt.

"Bradford, really?" Bradford was the neighbouring town, a ninety-minute drive away, not the sort of place you head to for a quick bite to eat. Maybe…Gabby's cheeks grew warm. Could Caleb have been serious at the bakery yesterday? Was dinner more than just dinner? Or was this just her getting her wires crossed? Well, whatever it was, she would enjoy her night out and not make anything of it. She would not over analyse, no matter what.

"Yeah, really. So just sit back, relax, and leave everything up to me."

They made a stop at the petrol station, Caleb going in to pay and returning with lightning speed, face flushed, hoping Gabby wouldn't ask him what the bulge was in his pocket, or what was in the bag he had just stashed in the boot. He felt like a teenager on his first date, the blue box catching his eye as he stood in line to pay for the petrol. He wasn't so cocky as to think that Gabby would fall into bed with him after a few kisses, but still, if anything did happen, it was his responsibility to protect her, protect them both, from the possibility of any repercussions. So, he had bought the box of condoms and had felt so self-conscious that he had whipped around the store throwing an assortment of items in his basket, including a blue energy drink, patterned bed socks, and a wind-up torch, although heaven knows what he needs with any of these items. Ten minutes later they had left Beryl Creek in the rear-view mirror.

CHAPTER TEN

Bradford was larger than Caleb had realised, something he was grateful about. It wasn't that he didn't want anyone to see them, he wasn't ashamed at being seen with Gabby, he just wanted them to have privacy. After he went home to Sydney, he didn't want there to be any awkward questions for Gabby to have to answer. He could spare her that at least. Not sure of where he was heading, Caleb drove around the outskirts of Bradford, getting a feel for the place. He was surprised to find that he actually liked it, he could well imagine himself coming back one day for a more leisurely visit. There were more than a handful of hotels to choose from, Caleb passing them all in an aimless circle, brooding on how best to bring up the subject with Gabby.

"Caleb?"

"Hmm," he turned left past a quaint bed and breakfast decked out in a bright yellow sunflower mural.

"We've been down this street five times already." Gabby sounded exasperated. "Can you just pick a hotel and park already?"

Stunned, Caleb pulled the car into the first free spot he found, wedged between a tree and a crumbling brick wall. He glanced over at Gabby, she smiled at him expectantly. "Gabby."

"Caleb."

"I was trying to find a way to ask you…I mean, I was hoping…I just thought…" He took a deep breath, turning and taking Gabby's hands in his own, his trademark sexy smile slowly unfurling across his face, dimples on full display. "Gabby, I am insanely attracted to you, for reasons that I can't fathom. It has been a long time since I have felt this way, and longer still since I have acted on it." He swallowed thickly, bringing her hands to his lips and kissing them softly. "I would be honoured if you would spend the night with me Gabby."

"You are nothing but trouble Caleb, the kind of trouble that could break a girl's heart. And yet…You leave me breathless." Gabby's fingers break free of Caleb's grasp and trail up to his cheek. "So, for tonight, let's pretend we are someone else." She tugs firmly on Caleb's collar, pulling him close, tilting her head upwards slightly to touch her lips against his.

Linking her hands behind his head, Gabby draws Caleb closer, uncaring of how forward she was being. It was about time that she did something for herself. It had been over ten years since Michael, since she had last been touched, kissed. She was out of her element with Caleb, she knew that. Michael had been selfish, in all aspects of their life together, not that she had noticed until after he had deserted her, a blessing in disguise, but he had been especially selfish in the bedroom. She had done what she had been told, nothing more, nothing less. Michael's main focus had always been himself; Gabby wasn't even sure he knew she was there half the time; he was so against her contributing in the bedroom in any way. A fission of excitement wove down Gabby's spine as Caleb nibbles his way down her jawline, she knew Caleb would not be a selfish lover. She broke away from him reluctantly.

"I would prefer not to do this here." Gabby's voice was huskier than she intended, an embarrassed blush tinting her cheeks, she was not used to speaking up for herself so much anymore these days.

"Then let's go." Caleb chuckled, starting the car and pulling back out into the traffic.

He pulled into the very next hotel they saw, a classic Georgian style building complete with white portico covered with bright bougainvillea, The Aurora. It screamed of wealth and privilege and carried an air of exclusivity. Perfect for spoiling Gabby. He tossed the keys to the valet, took Gabby by the elbow, and steered her inside. The roped-off section near the front door should have been Caleb's first clue, and it would have been, if he wasn't so obsessed with getting Gabby inside. The flash lit the scene perfectly, it really was a money shot for the photographer. The reclusive world-famous rockstar whispering deliciously into the ear of his mystery woman, Caleb could see the tabloid headlines already. Security guards rushed past the rope line, ushering the offending photographer away. Caleb knew it would do no good, he wasn't the only photographer who recognised Caleb. The manager checked them in himself, profoundly apologetic, promising to have champagne sent to their room at once by way of amends. Caleb flashed his publicity smile and assured him there was no harm done. Gabby looked bemused. As the door to their suite clicked shut behind them, she rounded on him, eyes narrowed slightly.

"Caleb, is it possible that you are more than just a music shop owner?"

"Ha! I wish," the lie tasted bitter to him, "I told you I came from money, my parents are fairly well known in Sydney, I can't speak for the photographer, but I imagine that the manager has heard of them. He is probably worried about bad press, which is ironic, my parents would never speak to the press under any circumstance." He took off his jacket and slung it over the arm of the sofa next to her bag, advancing on her slowly. "Anyway, I didn't come here to talk about me, or them, I came here to…" He brought his lips down to meet Gabby's, slowly, gently, relishing in the feel of her mouth on his, breaking away reluctantly. Gabby gathered the front of his shirt in her hands. "Gabby," Caleb groaned, moving away from her.

"What?" She rounded on him, snatching his hand back. "Did you think some photographer snapping random pictures would scare me away? I'm here. No strings attached okay? I'm not expecting you to stay any longer than you need to in Beryl Creek, I'm not looking for promises of forever Caleb." Gabby shrugged nonchalantly. "I want you," she finished forcefully, displaying more confidence than she knew she possessed.

"I want you too." Caleb cupped Gabby's face gently in both of his hands, rubbing the pad of his thumb across her lips, plump and kissable. His eyes never left hers, she blinked once, lips parted, the tip of her tongue darted across them. He didn't need any more encouragement. His lips crashed down on hers, his tongue probing her lips, asking, demanding, access. She gave it willingly. His fingers tangled in her hair and he angled her face, his tongue delving deeper inside, entering her mouth with confidence, tasting every inch he could, imprinting her on his memory. She tasted like sunshine and innocence, it danced on his tongue and spread along his nerve endings, warming him, reminding him of happier times. He had never wanted anybody as much as he wanted her right now

"Gabby, are you sure?" Caleb tore himself away from her mouth to ask. He had to know that this is what she wanted, really wanted, not something she wanted merely because she was caught up in a whirlwind of hormones and longing.

"I'm sure," Gabby pulled his mouth back down to hers, knowing he needed to hear her say the words.

She knew she wouldn't regret this night with Caleb, she had been alone for too long, it was time that she put herself first for a change, instead of putting herself and her needs and wants last. She had never done anything so reckless before in her life, she found it rather liberating. Maybe it was the fact that Caleb was only in Beryl Creek for a few more days, or maybe it was the electric undercurrents she felt whenever he was around. She sensed he was hiding something, there was a mysterious, a dangerous allure about him. Whatever the reason, Gabby wanted him, and judging by the bulge in his pants, he wanted her just as much. It was a powerful aphrodisiac, discovering that someone wanted you, that there was a physical and tangible reaction to the way someone felt about you. It was a heady concoction, one that Gabby had not experienced before. They were both consenting adults, why shouldn't they throw caution to the wind and have some fun.

Caleb pulled Gabby into his arms, his mouth meeting hers, tongues duelling for dominance, all reservations gone. He grew uncomfortably hard as she melted into the kiss, he needed her closer. He broke contact in order to strip off his shirt, easily dispensing with his shoes, kicking his jeans and boxer shorts off of his ankles, leaving them in a pile on the floor of the foyer. Naked, and completely at ease, he bent to scoop Gabby up into his arms, carrying her through the suite to the far end of the hall, where he could see the four-poster bed peeking out from behind the master bedroom doorway like a beacon. Placing her at the end of the large king-sized bed, he stripped her of her floral sundress, deftly removing her bra and panties, leaving her standing completely naked in front of him.

"Breathtaking," Caleb hungrily took her all in, she really was completely stunning. His eyes lingered on her breasts, full and luscious, a growl of satisfaction emanating from deep in his throat when her nipples puckered beneath his gaze. He drew her close, his mouth bending to enclose her puckered nipple, earning a deep satisfied groan from Gabby. He flicked his tongue over the peak, suckling and nipping it, grazing his teeth over the sensitive nub, causing Gabby to cry out and arch her back, thrusting her breasts towards him.

He moved to the other breast, showing it the same attention, angling Gabby slightly so that he had better access. His hand feathered a path down to her core between them, dipping his index finger inside her centre slowly, testing. He felt quite smug, feeling her wet core, knowing that he was responsible for that. As his finger continued to probe her silken folds, her wetness wrapped around him. He slid his finger out reluctantly, bringing it up to his mouth and tasting her on his tongue, delighting in the way her eyes rounded as she watched him. He moved his hand back to her core, tweaking her sensitive nub between his thumb and finger, feeling her writhe against him, trying to get closer to him, to his hand, whimpering with need. Caleb couldn't wait any longer, he wanted her now. Knowing she was ready for him, Caleb dropped to his knees, surprising Gabby. He slid his tongue in and out of her dripping core, flicking and tasting with each thrust, increasing his rhythm faster and faster, relishing the feel of her against his mouth, the sensation of her hips bucking against his face, the sounds of her moaning and screaming out his name as she came undone, shudders echoing through her body. Watching her fall apart at his hands was heady and made his need even more pressing. He stood and turned her around to face the bed, guiding her into the middle and bending her over, his hard length shuddering in anticipation as she went down willingly, sighing his name softly as she did.

Caleb took a moment to soak in the view, Gabby's legs were parted, buttocks high in the air as she supported the rest of her weight on her forearms on the bed. Her wetness glistened on her folds, and unable to resist, he bent his head to taste her again, a low groan escaping. She tasted so good, too good; she was addictive. He suckled her nub, still sensitive from her orgasm that had only just subsided, her body jerking in response as pleasure shot through her core. He slowly kissed her delicate folds as she mewed in delight, encouraging him. Needing no further urging, Caleb plunged his tongue deep inside Gabby's core again, drinking in her wetness, savouring her taste. He moaned into her, flicked his tongue over her nub and then drew back, straightening up. He needed more, he needed all of her, he needed to be buried deep inside her. Gripping his aching shaft in his hand, he used it as a guide to plunge his thick length deep into her from behind, a shout of triumph leaving his body as her walls stretched to accommodate his throbbing member with a delighted shout from Gabby.

Caleb held onto Gabby's hips, sliding an arm over the curve of her spine and around to her front, using his fingers to touch and tease her bundle of nerves as he moved inside her. Gabby urged him on with excited grunts and pleading, her hips thrusting as he moved in and out of her from behind, with exquisite slowness. He revelled in playing with her slick wetness with his fingers, relishing the very feel of her, rocking back and forth into her with long, slow, firm, deep strokes until he felt her climax building again. Caleb moved faster, he was frantic with need, so close to his release. He rocked Gabby in rhythm, fuelled on by her cries for him to go faster, harder, deeper until finally, they exploded together, Gabby's walls gripping Caleb's shaft tightly as he emptied his need deep inside of her, filling her, claiming her. As they collapsed on top of the bed, limbs entwined, totally spent, Caleb was struck with the thought that being with Gabby had felt like kismet or karma or whatever you wanted to call it. As they lay together, their breathing starting to return to normal, Caleb was struck with the realisation that despite his cringe-worthy petrol station stop, for the first time in his life, he had been too caught up in the moment to even think about using any protection.

CHAPTER ELEVEN

Swallowing his fear, Caleb pulled Gabby close, admitting his mistake, apologising. She fixed him with her softest smile, assuring him it would be okay, confessing that she was on the contraceptive pill to help regulate her cycle and that the chances of her actually falling pregnant were pretty slim. Not wanting to take any chances, she slid off the bed and dashed out of the room, returning with the box of condoms held triumphantly aloft in her hands above her head, like a warrior goddess returning from a hunt. Swinging his legs off the bed, Caleb pounced, capturing Gabby in his arms and twirling her around, tickling her sides until she laughingly relinquished the condoms, claiming his mouth in a searing kiss of victory that had Caleb growing hard again. Without breaking eye contact, Gabby slid the box of condoms from Caleb's hands, opening the packet and removing a row of foil-wrapped packages. Tearing one off and opening it, she slid it down his length. Caleb's hands cupped her buttocks, lifting her up, and she wrapped her legs around his waist, settling herself on to his erection.

He tethered her against the bedroom wall, hands holding her hips steady as he plunged in and out of her in a rhythm that had them both frantic with need. He angled her hips, withdrawing his length and plunging inside again, deeper and deeper, increasing his speed with each thrust. He knew she was close; he saw it in her eyes as his length plundered as deep inside her as was physically possible. There was no time for words, no soft whispers and gentle caresses, this time was primal, a raw need building between them that would only be sated by frantic thrusts and deep-seated grunts. Desire blazed in Gabby's eyes. Bodies slick with sweat, muscles clenched, cramped, spasmed. With a final twitch, he tipped her over the edge. Her eyes wide, Gabby clawed at his chest, biting into his shoulder and panting fast, dripping with need, lost in screams of pleasure and the heady scent of lust. Watching her come undone was all that he needed, and Caleb anchored her against his length as his orgasm ripped through him with a triumphant shout. They clung to each other, not daring to move, until their breathing returned to normal.

When they were both coherent again, they decided they were starving, Gabby declaring that she had never been so hungry before. They located the room service menu inside a folder next to the bed, and after studying it, simply ordered one of everything. While they waited for the food to arrive, they showered, separately at Gabby's request, not trusting herself to keep her hands off of Caleb, and dressed in oversized fluffy robes, snuggling down in front of the television to wait for their food. They didn't have long to wait, and they ate in comfortable silence, simply enjoying the peace with each other. Gabby watched Caleb over the rim of her champagne glass, quirking an eyebrow at the sight of his splayed legs, robe ajar, his erection on full display. The magnitude of his desire, so proudly on display, had her blushing. Setting his own glass aside, he advanced on her with hooded eyes, never breaking eye contact. Her tongue darted out to slide across her bottom lip, eyes darkening with lust, breasts heaving with her ragged breath, her body already quivering in anticipation.

Without preamble Caleb crushed her body to his, capturing her bottom lip between his teeth, biting down gently before sucking, his hand loosening the tie of the robe, letting it fall open. His hand snaked beneath the robe to cup her sex, feeling how wet she already was for him, her core pulsing with desire. He planted a trail of kisses down to her breast, latching onto it, suckling until her nipple puckered beneath his mouth. Rolling her hardened nib around in his mouth, Caleb flicked it with his tongue, nipping at it with his teeth as Gabby arched her back below him, his name a whimpered plea on her lips. Breaking away from her with a ragged breath, he ripped open a condom and sheathed himself before scooping her legs up over his shoulders, and plunging into her without preamble, sinking down into her deepness. Gabby gasped as Caleb stabbed into her, his length always surprised her, her body stretching to accommodate him. As she clung to him, her fingers gripping against his broad shoulders, his generous length grew even longer still as he stabbed into her shaking core again and again. Their release, when it came, was explosive, rolling spasms that anchored him inside her, their mutual shouts of triumph filling the air around them.

Gabby stroked Caleb's strong arms and back, splaying kisses across his chest, marvelling at the way he felt inside her, at the way he was already hard again. She shifted slightly, rolling them over so that Caleb's back was against the sofa and she was straddling him. With Caleb still buried deep inside of her throbbing core, Gabby took one of his hands, guiding it up to her sensitive nub, humming appreciatively as he began to swirl and roll it between his thumb and forefinger, pulling it lightly, then pinching it with a sharp twist, shooting spasms of pleasure to her very core, causing her to jerk and rock atop him. Splaying her legs even wider, Gabby arched her back, leaning backwards to hold on to Caleb's calves, giving him an uninterrupted view of her straddling him to the hilt, his balls flanking either side of her molten centre. Caleb knew that no matter how long he lived, he would never see anything hotter than what he was seeing right now. Mesmerised, he raised his free hand to twist and pinch her pebbled nipple in time with the ministrations to her sensitive nub.

Gabby's entire body was tingling with delight, humming with a need only Caleb could satisfy. She knew they were close, she wanted to see his face, to see what she could do to him. As his hand continued to torment her breast, Gabby delighted in the sensations he elicited from her peaked nipples. Hesitantly, she reached down between them to touch his balls, a gasp escaping Caleb's lips as he bucked unexpectedly beneath her, plunging even deeper into her.

"Yes, Gabby, oh, that was so hot," Caleb gasped out, releasing her nipple and her sensitive nub, gripping on to her hips instead, tethering her to him, keeping her seated firmly on his erection. Gabby moved her hips in small circles, rolling his balls in her hot hands, her nub rubbing against Caleb's pelvic bone, fissions of heat coiling up her body. When he was almost at climax, Gabby released Caleb's balls, looked him straight in the eye, slipped her hand in between their bodies and gave her nub a hard tweak, shooting spasms of pleasure to her very core, sending them both over the edge with such force she was sure her heart had stopped beating. Completely spent, Caleb held her as they rested, curled into each other, bodies entwined.

It was close to midnight when they finally unravelled from each other's arms, Caleb taking Gabby's hand and leading her out onto the covered patio, not bothering to put a light on, the moon overhead cast a soft glow, gently illuminating the patio furniture. Gabby sat on a sun lounge, oddly self-conscious despite the late hour, while Caleb walked across to the railing to peer up at the stars.

"There is magic in the air tonight Gabby," Caleb's whisper floated to her on the gentle evening breeze.

"Magic? I like that, and here was I, thinking it was just lust." Crossing over to Gabby, he lowered himself onto the sun lounger beside her, gently cupping her breast as he lowered his head to claim her mouth. "Caleb!" Gabby's voice was thick with need. "We can't, what if someone sees us?"

"We can," he nibbled at her bottom lip, giving her nipple a quick twist between his thumb and forefinger, causing her to cry out in surprise. "It's the middle of the night Gabby, there are no lights on anywhere, who is going to see us? I want to feel you wrapped around me, I want to bury myself deep inside you."

She splayed her hands over his chest, absently pinching and plucking at his nipples, sighing in delight as he leant into her, deepening their kiss. It was Gabby who broke the kiss, pushing firmly against Caleb's chest, until he sat up, confusion clouding his eyes. Her lips were swollen, nipples pebbled with aching need. Caleb watched, eyes darkening with lust as Gabby lazily let her legs fall open, never breaking eye contact, giving him a perfect view of her silky folds waiting for him. Manoeuvring to kneel between her legs, Caleb wasted no time, the head of his throbbing length twitching, teasing her sensitive bundle of nerves, Gabby's hips bucking beneath him in an attempt to get closer to him, to draw his throbbing member inside her aching folds. With deliberate slowness, Caleb slid into Gabby's soft centre, savouring the moans he elicited from her, loving the way his name sounded on her lips. He slowly built up a steady rhythm, matched thrust for thrust by Gabby, until, with a final thrust, he tipped them over the abyss, his triumphant shout mingling with Gabby's fevered calling of his name.

Caleb was worried. He had been intimate with Gabby for less than six hours, but it already felt like a lifetime. Time had moved at a different speed here tonight, with them. The thought of tomorrow coming and ending this thing that they had between them tonight was unsettling for Caleb, it was a new experience for him. he had never been clingy in any past relationships, had never wanted to be, and had certainly never encouraged that in any of his other lovers. He was starting to wonder if he could walk away from her, if he would. He couldn't stay, not with the lie that was between them in any case. And yet, if he left, what would he be returning to? An empty house, a stalled career, an estranged family.

CHAPTER TWELVE

Gabby could hear the lulling sound of Caleb's solid heartbeat, her fingers tracing random patterns across his chest and down his sides.

"Why did you come to Beryl Creek?"

"Hmm?" Caleb wasn't sure if Gabby had actually spoken or if her voice had been a hallucination.

"Why did you come to Beryl Creek?" Gabby pushed herself up on her elbow to look down at Caleb. He wanted to pretend he hadn't heard, wanted to fire off some quick lie, but he was unable to speak. Nothing came to him. His fingers twitched, if he just reached out and tweaked her nipple slightly, she would be writhing back underneath him, or maybe on top of him if he was lucky. He sighed deeply, no, that wasn't fair, he wasn't going to fob her off with sex, no matter how mind-blowing an experience it was. Maybe he could tell her the truth. Maybe he should tell her the truth. They had no future, he didn't owe her anything, if it stunned her, if it had her despising him, then so be it.

"My brother died; I am avoiding his memorial."

"What?" Gabby couldn't believe it, Caleb's brother was dead, that's why he was in Beryl Creek. "Oh Caleb, I am so sorry," she reached down to stroke his cheek gently.

"I don't need your sympathy," Caleb scoffed, brushing her hand away. He saw the sting of rejection flash in her eyes, felt slightly guilty for being rude. He knew he had to push her away, it was for her own good, if no other reason. "You want to know why I am here? My brother died, I killed him," Caleb choked on the words, "The only reason he is dead right now is because of me. I haven't seen my family in nearly twelve months, they have a memorial service planned for my brother, so I came to Beryl Creek instead, until after the service, then I will go back to Sydney."

"Caleb…" Gabby trailed off, she knew what raw pain sounded like, could see right through his tough indifference. "I don't believe that you are responsible, and I don't think you do either, not really. I think you are in pain and blaming yourself is a whole lot easier than blaming your bother." It was like a slap in the face for Caleb.

"You think I blame Sam? I don't, I blame myself. If I hadn't…" Caleb stopped midsentence.

"Sam? That was your brother?" Gabby probed gently.

"Yes," Caleb sighed, paused to take a deep breath before continuing. "Sam, Samuel, was my older brother. He was my best friend actually; it had always been just the two of us against the world. While my sisters were busy playing dolls and tea parties, Sam and I would plot world domination," Caleb's voice was thick with emotion. "It will be a year ago that he died, a year ago next week."

"What happened?" Caleb knew the question would come. Eventually someone, somewhere was bound to ask him. It didn't hurt any less that it was Gabby instead of a nameless reporter looking for a juicy scoop.

"He was killed in a car crash."

"A car crash? Oh my God, Caleb…That's what you meant. You told dad that you haven't played the guitar since you had an accident…Caleb, were you in the car too?" He heard the horror in her voice, the underlying fear, dread.

"Yes, we were both in the car. I lived, he died, someone's idea of a cruel joke, a cosmic error." Caleb didn't mean for it to sound so cold, but that was the truth. Sam was dead and it should have been Caleb instead.

"Caleb, surely you don't think…" Gabby swallowed uncertainly, not sure how to continue, or if she even should.

"He was so much better at everything than I was. It should not have been him. I had already had a full life, but Sam, he was only getting started. He was a lawyer, he had just made partner in his law firm. A good, stable, solid profession. I wanted to go out, there was a party at a local nightclub, and I wanted to go. I wanted Sam to come along, I wanted him to loosen up, to see my world, to watch me work my magic with the ladies." At this Gabby snorted. "I told him that he needed to relax more and work less. He wasn't interested, he had a big case to prepare for, but I badgered and badgered him until he agreed. If I had just listened to him, had just let him be, he would still be here today. It replays in here," Caleb tapped the side of his head, "over and over, on a continuous torturous loop."

Laughing, Caleb turned to look at Sam, his eyes twinkling. "See," he couldn't help teasing, "I knew you would have a good time tonight Sammy."

"I always have a good time with you little brother," Sam ruffled Caleb's perfectly lacquered hair, deliberately squashing the rock star 'ruffled fresh from bed' style that Caleb had spent hours perfecting. "But we can't all be irresponsible rockstars now, can we? Some of us actually have to work to earn a living!" It was the same banter that always existed between them, the ribbing and poking fun laced with the love that comes from being a family.

"Work?!" snorted Caleb, "Ha! As if! You're a partner in a law firm Sammy, how much work can you possibly do? Don't you have staff?" Caleb's raucous laugh mingled with Sam's deep chortle.

"Staff? That's your department brother dear, how many do you have now? Eighteen? Ninete-"

"Watch out!" Caleb's panicked shout interrupts Sam, and he blinks once, surprise etching his features. The unrelenting screech of bare metal tyre rims on bitumen reaches a crescendo before fading into silence, the world turning black, the only sound an incessant beep, beep, beep.

"I woke up three weeks later in intensive care. Sam had bled out at the scene, a passer-by had found us, they had to pry our hands apart in order to cut me from the car. Some teenagers had thought it would be a fun prank to play to dress up a mannequin as a small child and place it in the middle of the road. Smart as they were, they fled the scene of the crash, leaving their mobile phone behind. They had filmed the entire thing. I missed the funeral," Caleb couldn't breathe, bile rising up in his throat as he pushed the memory away.

"Oh Caleb," her eyes, full of compassion, was his undoing, a sob renting the air, finally breaking free after all this time. She pulled him close, holding him tightly as his sobs of pain and anguish filled the air. She sat like that for minutes, hours, she wasn't sure, simply stroking his hair, thinking. She sensed a shift in him before he moved, a stillness, a peace, had come over him. she wondered if he had ever cried over Sam before now, somehow, she doubted it, not if he blamed himself for his brother's death.

Caleb fixed her with a long stare, before gathering her up into his arms, carrying her into the bedroom and sitting her on the edge of the bed. He cupped her breasts and started to knead them, watching as they pebbled under his intense gaze almost immediately. Bowing his head, his mouth catches a nipple, and he sucks hard, eliciting a surprised gasp from Gabby. He rests a knee between her thighs on the bed, the shifting weight dipping the bed, Gabby's breasts bouncing free and unhindered, begging to be touched. His arm snaked around her back, supporting her, his tongue darted out, flicking across her hardened nipple, suckling and nipping at it with his teeth. His hand trailed down to the apex of her thighs, he knew he would find her wet to the touch, he knew if he slid two fingers inside her silky folds, he would feel her pool of wetness wrap around him, encasing him, covering him in her juices. Instead, he fell to his knees, and leant forwards, tasting her wetness, his tongue probing her core, her eyes round as she watched him. Caleb could feel Gabby writhing against his mouth, trying to get closer, whimpering with need. Knowing she was ready for him, he guided her knees up and over his shoulders, giving him a perfect view of her silky folds. Knowing that he was responsible for her obvious wetness only highlighted his ache, his member growing uncomfortable, making his need even more urgent.

With a low growl, Caleb dipped his head, tongue plunging deep inside, licking, sucking, tasting Gabby's delicate folds. Gabby fevered with delight, encouraging him, Caleb's hard length shuddering in anticipation as she sighed his name. Reaching between them, Gabby's hand found his rigid shaft, gripping it tightly, pumping him firmly up and down, slowly at first, before increasing with speed, the heat and friction of her hand against his member the sweetest of torture. Jerking upright, Caleb captures her hand in his own, removing it from his engorged length, guiding it up over her head and holding it there. With a single thrust, his thick shaft enters deep into her softness, her walls stretching to accommodate his length with a delighted triumphant shout from Gabby. His need urgent, Caleb thrusts deeper, harder, Gabby moving in sync with him, thrusting her hips to draw him deeper inside her centre. Caleb moves faster, so close to his release, Gabby moaning and screaming out his name. Their release is mutual, Gabby gripping Caleb's shoulders, shudders echoing through her body as he emptied his need deep inside of her, filling her, before collapsing atop her on the bed.

Gabby wasn't sure how long they stayed this way, clinging to each other, Caleb's shaft already starting to stir again in anticipation, in need. He was insatiable, a fact which delighted her. He was also very dangerous, addictive even, she reminded herself cautiously. She wondered if she would ever tire of him, of having him buried deep inside of her, of the way her body felt wrapped around his? He fit inside of her so perfectly, and the things he did, the unselfish way in which he gave her pleasure, if she was stupid, she would go ahead and pin her hopes on Caleb. But she wasn't, she reminded herself firmly, she wasn't stupid, she was smart, and she was a realist. She had tonight, and that was enough, it would have to be, no matter how much soul-baring he did while he looked at her with those wounded puppy dog eyes.

CHAPTER THIRTEEN

"Gabby!" Caleb gasped, as her hand slipped between his legs, taking a firm grip on his shaft and starting to slide her hand up and down. After their previous joining, Caleb had shared with Gabby stories of Sam, and Gabby had listened, commenting from time to time. The love Caleb had for Sam was palpable, and as the night stretched on, Gabby urged Caleb to go home, to speak to his mother, to attend Sam's memorial.

"You need closure Caleb, and I would imagine that your parents do as well. It wasn't your fault, Caleb, you are hurting your family by blaming yourself, by keeping yourself from them. Your parents didn't just lose Sam, did they, Caleb? They lost you as well that night." He knew she was right, he had known for some time now that he would have to go back, to face his family, to face a final goodbye to Sam.

"I will think about it tomorrow, for right now all I want, all I need, is you." He pulled Gabby close.

"Caleb," she took his mouth in her own, "you have me." Gabby shimmied down the bed, stopping when she found her prize. "You are so gorgeous," breathed Gabby, marvelling at Caleb's erect member, just as chiselled as she had imagined it would be.

Eyes never leaving his face, Gabby trailed her fingers up his inner thighs, softly caressing, before taking a delicate testicle into her mouth, causing Caleb to cry out in surprise. Gabby sucked gently, rolling his aching testicle around her tongue, releasing it with a soft nip, before repeating the same ministrations to the other testicle. Rock hard, and standing erect, Caleb wasn't sure how much longer he would last, his hand moving down with the intention of releasing his need. Slapping his hand away, still not breaking eye contact, Gabby shifted her mouth to his aching shaft, her tongue darting around the rim and over the top, fingers tickling the underside. She slid her waiting mouth over his hardened length, drawing him deep inside. Watching Gabby slide her mouth up and down his length, Caleb decided, was one of the hottest things he had ever seen. Gabby's teeth grazed along his length as she slid her mouth up and down his shaft, painstakingly slowly, before building up a rhythm, faster and faster, before slowing back down, determined to draw out his pleasure for as long as she could.

"Gabby, I won't last much longer, I'm going to come!" Caleb ground out; his voice impatient with need. "I can't…hold on…much longer!" Gabby merely took Caleb's shaft even deeper into her mouth, humming as she did, sending vibrations shooting down his length. "Gabby!" Caleb cried out triumphantly as his orgasm tore through his body. He was vaguely aware of Gabby licking him clean before kissing his swollen head, but beyond that, he was incapable of coherent thought.

"Your turn," Caleb growled, having regained his composure. Pulling her flush against his erection, he captured one of her pink nipples in his mouth. It stunned him, his attraction to her, his primal need to have her, the way a single look from her had him coming undone. He plunged a finger deep into her core, rewarded with her excited moan and an unexpected buck of her hips. He slid his finger in and out of her, enjoying the feeling of her becoming wetter and wetter under his ministrations, until his need for her became more pressing, and he pulled back, looking at her flushed face. Gabby wiggled delightedly against him, the thick head of his erection rubbing against her sensitive nub. She reached her hands up and guided his mouth back down to her nipples, relishing the sensations he elicited from her. Moaning softly, she rolled them over, surprising Caleb by straddling him and giving him a delicious view of her heavy breasts. Smiling lazily, she leant over his chiselled chest to kiss him deeply, her nipples grazing against his firm chest. His hands glided down her sides, cupping her bottom and pressing her firmly against his erection. Gabby moved her hips in small circles as she deepened the kiss, her nub rubbing against Caleb's hard length, teasing him slowly, gasping and jerking away from his mouth when his hand slipped in between them and gave her nub a hard tweak, shooting spasms of pleasure to her very core.

Straightening up, with Caleb's hand still kneading and rolling her nub between his fingers, Gabby took a condom from the dresser and unwrapped it, rolling it down Caleb's shaft, then, with a wink, she grasped Caleb's erection, using her hand to guide his throbbing length deep inside of her aching centre. Caleb watched in fascination as Gabby slowly slid down the length of his shaft, almost all the way, and then slid back up again, torturously slowly, with a wicked smile on her gorgeous face. Desperate with need and unable to stand the wait any longer, Caleb released her nub, before reaching up and grabbing hold of her hips, pulling her all the way down on his shaft in one swift move, drawing a surprised gasp from Gabby's parted lips. Caleb nearly came undone as he watched his shaft disappear completely into Gabby's centre, feeling her muscles stretch to accommodate his size. She was mesmerising, he decided as he watched her arch her back, flinging her head back as she sung his name, taking him deeper still.

He started to move inside her, his eyes feasting on the sight of her, hypnotised by the way her breasts swayed and danced for him as she met and rode every one of his thrusts, the way she threw her head back in a scream of triumph as she orgasmed atop of him, bucking her hips as her release tore through her. Gripping his hips, Gabby called his name, tipping him over the edge and grinding down onto him until his spasms stopped, collapsing onto his chest with a contented sigh. Caleb had never been more spent in his life, or more turned on. Being with Gabby was a heady experience that he was fast becoming addicted to, with her, everything just felt right, even the way her luscious breasts currently felt against his chiselled chest was exactly as it should be.

Gabby woke to the feel of Caleb's fingers dancing along her spine, early morning sunlight streaming in through the curtains. She rolled over slowly and stretched, smiling up at Caleb shyly, a blush starting to creep along her cheekbones, the memory of last night lingering in the air between them. She ached in places she didn't even know existed. Gabby was floored by Caleb's stamina, he never seemed to tire of her, sexually. They had barely slept, heck, they had barely let go of each other, thirsting to discover each other, to touch, to taste, to delight in exploration of attraction. Caleb's gaze raked over her body, slowly, deliberately. Her blush deepened. Gabby looked around for the sheet, a tangled mess of fabric balled up on the floor.

"You are breathtaking." Caleb drew Gabby close, claiming her mouth with a fiery kiss that would be forever seared into her memory. His hand slid down to her centre, his length growing uncomfortably hard when his slender fingers discovered Gabby already wet, waiting, for him.

Shifting slightly, Caleb pushed Gabby's knees up, watching as she slowly lowered them, dropping them to her sides. She was completely open for him. Splayed out, he could see each one of her silky folds, the ripest of peaches, waiting for his mouth. Caleb groaned in pleasure; she would be the death of him. He dipped his head, flicking, teasing her sensitive nub with his tongue, claiming it with his mouth and sucking gently, as she writhed beneath him, gasping his name on her lips. He turned his attentions to her silky folds, glisteningly wet, begging for Caleb's touch. His tongue slid inside slowly, deliberately teasing her, tasting her juices. Caleb continued to slide his tongue in and out of Gabby's core, flicking her nub with his fingers, pinching, rolling it between his thumb and forefinger as she bucked her hips beneath him, her breathing growing shallow.

"Caleb!" she pleaded, her hips bucking, "please!"

"Please what? Tell me what you need." He grinned wickedly. He wanted to hear her say it. He wanted to see her come undone at his hands, by his mouth, he wanted to know that it was his doing.

"I want you. Inside me. Now!" She growled her demand fiercely. Caleb smiled, reaching over to the bedside table for a condom, he unwrapped it, slipping it on. After their first-time last night, he had been certain to use protection, he had promised Gabby he wouldn't hurt her and as far as he was concerned, that also meant protecting her against any unwanted consequences. Caleb rose to his knees, leaning over Gabby and using her knees as support, he drove his rigid length into her, before pulling out fully and stabbing in again and again. Gabby arched her back and bucked her hips to meet Caleb's powerful thrusts, screaming with incoherent pleasure as he drove in harder and deeper, his thick member hitting the wall of her cervix.

"Caleb, oh my god, Caleb, yes, yes!" Gabby didn't hold back as he moved within her, encouraging him with her gasps and moans, urging him deeper with her grunted words.

"Come for me," Caleb ordered, knowing she was close. Pulling his length out fully, he gave one final thrust all the way into her core, and felt her walls tighten around his stiffened member as he pushed her over the edge, hearing her scream out his name with wild abandon. With one final thrust he exploded inside her, gripping her hips for support, until totally spent, he collapsed beside her.

CHAPTER FOURTEEN

She needed to move, she couldn't put it off any longer, goodness knew what time it was, her parents were probably worried, either that or they would now be well worn out from looking after Lucia and Sofia. She stretched out, her arm reaching for Caleb, grasping at air, his side of the bed nothing but empty space. Huh. As if on cue, Caleb walked through the bedroom doorway, grasping two steaming mugs in front of him.

"Good morning sleepy head." He passed her a mug. "I may have found a state-of-the-art coffee machine in the kitchen cupboard."

"Good morning," she accepted the mug eagerly, sipping the hot liquid carefully. "You made me a cappuccino?" She smiled up at him.

"No," he looked sheepish. "I couldn't work out how to get the darn machine to switch on, so I gave up and called room service." She laughed at this, a warm, sunshiny laugh that floated around Caleb and coiled in his heart. "Gabby," he reached for her hand.

"Caleb," her voice held a soft warning. "Don't. Don't say it, let's just leave it as it is, okay? I had a wonderful time last night, and this morning, and it is something that I will never forget, we don't need to say anything else. A single night, a memory, that was all it ever was, was all it ever could be. Now it is time to head back to reality, for both of us Caleb. Me to the girls and my life in Beryl Creek, you to your family, to your music shop, maybe even to your guitar playing." She nudged gently. Cupping his cheek, she placed a soft kiss on his lips, lingering ever so slightly. "I am so happy to have known you, Caleb, to have spent time with you, thank you, for this, for last night, for everything." She swung her legs off the bed. "I'm going to have a shower; I won't be long." As he watched her walk away Caleb was full of a sense of foreboding. He knew she was right, reality was calling, they had to go back. He just wished it didn't have to be so soon.

The drive back to Beryl Creek from Bradford was quiet, subdued, both Caleb and Gabby lost in their own thoughts. He glanced at her and smiled, thrilled when she returned it. She was going to be a hard act to follow, that was even supposing that he wanted anyone else to follow. Truthfully, he wasn't so sure. He had managed twelve months without needing anyone to bed, perhaps he simply wasn't interested? Or maybe Gabby had been the one to break the dam, and now he would be back to normal, whatever that was, happily taken a different woman to bed each night of the week, not caring what other people thought? It was a sobering thought, one that did not sit well with Caleb. He didn't want people to think that of him, he didn't want to think that way of himself, he didn't want to be that way, not now, not after Gabby, not anymore. He pushed all thoughts of the future aside, he still had two more days in Beryl Creek, two more days with Gabby and her family, he was going to make them last.

By the time they arrived at the camel races the sun was already high in the sky. Gabby had texted her father to find out where they had parked Maria's minivan, and they were now trawling the carpark looking for a space nearby. One opened up two cars down and Caleb patiently waited for the driver to reverse, before sliding in and cutting the engine. Caleb and Gabby wandered through the gate, and down to the spot they used yesterday, Maria and Nico being creatures of habit, it was easy to spot them. Lucia and Sofia mobbed Caleb and Gabby, both talking at once, relating every little thing that had happened in the past eighteen hours. Anyone would think that Gabby had been away for weeks instead of a single night. Nico greeted them enthusiastically, filling them on the camel heats that had taken place earlier that day, while Maria sat in her chair, lips pressed firmly together in a tight line, very obviously unimpressed. Gabby tried to engage Maria in conversation, but soon gave up and flopped down on the blanket next to the girls, who were comparing their camels and trying to decide if either of them would win.

Caleb wasn't sure if it was just him, but the afternoon seemed to really drag by, until, finally, with a last whoosh of hooves and an insane amount of dust, All Bets Off crossed the finish line to take out first place. Her rider couldn't have looked more unlike a camel racer if she had tried to. A heavyset forty-five-year-old local woman, Annie Sinclair worked as a primary school teacher during the day, only entering the camel race as a dare, egged on by her husband Darren, the local post office clerk. Darren had been giving her a hard time over her fear of camels for years, this was the perfect way to get him to eat a slice of humble pie. She stole the camel cup from last year's winner, John Walsh, who came in second and didn't seem to care at all. As wind-down musicians take to the stage, Caleb again helps the Bianchi's to pack up their belongings, and as a higglety pigglety group they sashay down the ghost gum-studded trail that ushers visitors from the park. As they pass Sascha, Gabby and her embrace, lifelong friends, having bonded over shared tales. As the sun dips down in the sky, a soft breeze ruffles Caleb's hair, the sounds of camels moaning can be heard from the pens nearby. It is time to go.

As Caleb followed Maria's car through the main street of Beryl Creek, something didn't seem right. It was far too busy, even for a Sunday afternoon.

"Does there seem like a lot of cars in town today?"

"Hmm? It is probably just leftover tourists from the camel cup, enjoying a meal and a cold beer before heading back to Sydney or some other town. Why? You don't like crowds?" Gabby teased gently.

"I don't like accidents that can be caused by crowds," he corrected her.

"It is fine Caleb," Gabby fixed him with a thoughtful stare. "This is a small town, anytime there are more than a dozen cars parked in the main street it looks like an invasion of tourists, we are nearly home, it will be okay." The further they drove; the more paranoid Caleb became. He could have sworn that the publican had pointed and stared as they drove past. It must just be his guilty conscious, there was no way that anyone knew he had spent the night with Gabby, no way at all.

As they turned down Gabby's street, Caleb knew he hadn't been imagining anything at all. There, camped outside her house, were a dozen media vans, covering all the major television networks. A swarm of paparazzi had Maria's car surrounded, Caleb could tell from here that Lucia and Sofia were scared, not sure of which way to look.

"Darn them!" Caleb growled, slamming his brakes on and screeching to a stop at the curb.

"Caleb, what on Earth?"

"Get the door unlocked now," Caleb ordered without looking back at her. "I'll get everybody else." Gabby had no idea what was going on, but she knew now was not the time to argue with Caleb. She flung open the car door and sprinted up the sidewalk to the front door, throwing her arm up across her face to shield her eyes from the multitude of bombarding flashes that were currently going off in her face. Finally, the key turned, and she shoved the door open with a firm push, wishing that she had insisted that Bella be allowed to stay inside. She would have been a handy deterrent right about now.

Caleb slipped in behind her, slamming the front door, Lucia and Sofia each gripping tightly to one of his hands. "Here, take the girls, I'm going back to help your parents inside," he spun on his heel and was out of the door and down the walkway before Gabby had time to respond.

"Here, quickly, go through into the lounge room. Don't open the curtains, okay? We don't want anyone taking photos inside the house. I'm going to call the police, don't move until I get off the phone." She kissed them each quickly, giving them a squeezy hug, before crossing into the office and snatching the phone up out of its cradle. Whoever these people were, they had no right to be taking photos of her house, or of her or the girls for that matter, and she intended to have them arrested. The phone was answered by the local police station on the third ring, one of the benefits of living in a small-town Gabby supposed. Gabby explained the situation to Hank, the officer in charge and one of her old school friends, and he promised to have every unit on the way to her house by the time she disconnected the phone call. Gabby didn't doubt him, he had always been a man of his word.

Gabby had just hung up the telephone as Caleb wheeled her father through the door, her mother dashing in after them, shutting the door with a loud crack.

"What the hell is going on? Gabby, what happened?" Maria looked frazzled, flopping down on the sofa next to Lucia and Sofia, pulling them close for a cuddle.

"Girls, go upstairs please, I want you to play quietly in your room, you can watch the television if you would like to, I want to talk to your grandparents for a little while okay? I will call you when you can come back downstairs again." Sofia and Lucia went willingly, it wasn't very often they were allowed to watch television in their room, and they were eager to get upstairs and decide on a show they both liked. Once the sounds of their running feet had reached their bedroom upstairs, Gabby turned to Caleb, arms crossed over her chest. "Yesterday at Bradford, there was a photographer there, did you know that he was going to be there?"

"A photographer? Gabby, what are you talking about, why would there be a photographer?" Maria was confused.

"Mum, please, I need Caleb to answer."

"What? No, how can you even think that?"

"How can I think that? Are you serious right now? Caleb, there was a photographer last night, he took your photo, mine too by the way. I asked you about it, and what did you say? You told me that your parents were wealthy, that they were well known in their social circle. Was that the truth?"

"Mostly." Caleb wished he was anywhere else, wished that Gabby would stop looking at him with accusations in her eyes.

"Mostly. Caleb, what does that mean?" Her eyes narrowed. "You know why the press is camped outside, don't you? Just how wealthy are your parents Caleb, how well known?"

"It isn't my parents, it is me." He admitted quietly, waiting for a reaction. He didn't have to wait long, all three pairs of eyes coming to rest on his face. He tried not to fidget, tried not to twitch, tried to remain outwardly calm, but knew he was fast running out of time, that stalling was not going to work for much longer.

"What do you mean? You're rich?" Gabby sounded so unsure, it made Caleb want to laugh. He found it refreshing, he couldn't remember the last time someone had been unaffected by the fact he was rich.

"Rich, sort of," Caleb smiled. "I'm a multi-millionaire Gabby."

"You're a what?" Gabby felt faint, Caleb had lied to her.

"A multi-millionaire. Have you heard of the band The Three Odd Lizards?" Gabby nodded mutely, she knew that Lucia and Sofia listened to them frequently. "Well, that is me. I'm Caleb Roman, the lead guitarist. That is why the press is outside right now. That is why my photograph was taken last night, although I swear to god Gabby, that was not planned, and I had no idea that they would be there. Had I known; I would never have taken you there." As soon as the words left his mouth Caleb realised his error.

"You would never have taken me there? Really Caleb, why not? Too embarrassing for you to be seen with me is it?"

"Gabby, it's not like that, honestly, let me explain."

"Answer me this Caleb. Did you deliberately lie to me, to my family?"

"Yes. No, it wasn't like that", Caleb sounded desperate, even to his ears.

"Then how was it Caleb?"

"I needed to get away, my house is nothing but memories, I didn't want to be there. I needed to go somewhere where I could just sit and think. When I arrived, no one seemed to recognise me, it was…Refreshing. So, I didn't tell anyone who I was, but I didn't lie either Gabby, I told you my name."

"You said you owned a music shop." Nico helpfully added to the conversation.

"And I do," Caleb affirmed. "It just isn't my main job," Caleb confessed sheepishly. "I'm sorry, I honestly thought that no one would ever find out. I would never have come to Beryl Creek, would never have stayed here with you guys if I ever thought that there was any possibility of me being discovered. I have spent the last twelve months in seclusion, in hiding, that I selfishly thought it was my new reality, I never considered that the press would still be interested in my whereabouts. I'm sorry."

There was a knock on the front door, Gabby opening it against her parents' wishes, to find Hank standing there, smiling warmly.

"Hank, come in," Gabby swung the door open wide, beckoning him in.

"Gabby, no, thank you. I just wanted to let you know that I have issued all of the press personnel with trespass notices and moved them all along. I'm sorry that I can't run them out of town for you", Hank smiled, "I understand that they are all staying up at the caravan park tonight, possibly longer. I just wanted to let you know. I can post a car outside tonight if you would like me to, otherwise, I can get the guys to drive past on their rounds, make sure none of the press tries to sneak back onto the property if you would like me to?"

"Thank Hank, that would be great. Do you think it's likely?"

"Honestly? No, they seem to be content to wait it out until he shows his face again," Hank gestures to Caleb, not sure of who he was or what the big deal was.

"Okay, thanks Hank, we appreciate it," Gabby showed him to the door, waving until his car and turned the corner.

CHAPTER FIFTEEN

"You did this Caleb; it is your fault they are here in Beryl Creek. Are we going to have our photo's on the cover of tomorrow's newspaper?" It was a fair question.

"No, Gabby, it won't be on the cover of tomorrow's newspaper," Caleb took a deep breath before continuing. "The photographs will be in every single newspaper and magazine in the country, as well as on every single television network and news outlet, both locally and internationally. Not just tomorrow morning, but for every single day, from now until the day I give them a more interesting or scandalous story to report on. I'm sorry, I should never have involved you."

"No, you shouldn't have. So here is what is going to happen now. You are going to fix this Caleb; you are going to fix this mess tonight. And then first thing tomorrow morning you are going to leave. I don't care where you go or what you do, but I want you out of this house, is that understood?"

"Gabby," his voice sounded strained, hoarse. "Please, don't do this, we can work this out, let me explain-"

"No Caleb. I don't want to hear any more lies from you. Every single thing you told me was a lie, every single thing. Don't talk to me anymore."

Caleb watched Gabby walk out of the room with a sinking feeling in the pit of his stomach. He wanted to go after her, to chase her, to make her listen to him, but he knew it was of no use, she had already made up her mind. A part of him agreed with her. Maria and Nico watched him carefully, there was a sad expression on Nico's face, a puzzled one on Maria's. Caleb knew that he had to fix this, the Bianchi's were good people, they didn't deserve to be harassed by the press just because they had the misfortune to take him in and to include him in their lives for a short while. Caleb was resigned to what he had to do, but that didn't make it any easier. Sitting on the sofa, he pulled out his mobile phone, scrolling through his contacts until he saw the familiar name, hesitating for a moment before hitting the call button.

"Hello." The steadying voice of his agent answered almost immediately, momentarily transporting Caleb to another time and place.

"Tom, it's Caleb, I need a favour." It was a testament to how much people loved him, that when Caleb reached out to his agent, there were no questions, no demands for explanations, no admonitions. There was only concern.

"Name it."

"I came up to Beryl Creek for a couple of weeks, to clear my head before, ah, Sam's," Caleb cleared his throat self-consciously, "memorial service. No one here knew who I was, or if they did, they certainly didn't say anything about it. The only thing is, someone found out, a reporter at the Bradford last night. I was there with a friend, Gabby, the lady who runs the bed and breakfast that I am staying at. Anyway, her family and I have just gotten back to her bed and breakfast, and there is media camped out everywhere, all up and down the street, photographers, reporters, television crews, you name it, they are here on her front lawn. She has two little girls, a father who is sick, I don't want this on the news, I don't want anyone harassing them."

"I'll take care of it." As relieved as Tom was that Caleb had finally contacted him, he knew they had very limited time to get on top of the story. Any questions that he had for Caleb would simply have to wait, he had damage control to do, starting with a courtesy phone call to Caleb's parents, Judy and Peter. Tom knew that Caleb had not been in touch with his parents for many months, and he also knew that if Judy and Peter saw this media circus on the television news or in the tabloids before they had been warned, they would be very upset. More than that, they would be distressed, worried for their son. Tom knew that their reasons for worry were justified, a part of Caleb had also died in the crash alongside his brother that night, and there were those in the industry who doubted that Caleb would ever fully recover. Tom had more faith in Caleb than that, which was why he had been so supportive in giving Caleb the space he needed, to heal, to mourn. Initially, it had been expected that Caleb would take the rest of the year off, three months at most, but that soon became six months and then eight months, and now it had been almost a full twelve months. This had been the first Tom had heard from Caleb in months, and he chose to see it as a step in the right direction.

"Peter? It's Tom, I just wanted to let you know that Caleb has just called me." Peter answered on the fourth ring, slightly out of breath.

"Caleb, oh my gosh, I'll get Judy, she'll be so-"

"Peter wait!" Tom cut him off before he could call Judy. As much as Tom loved Judy, she would be tearful, and he really didn't have the time to allay all of her fears right now. "I don't have time, I'm sorry, I wish that I did. Listen, Caleb's got trouble with the press, I need to get off the phone in order to run interference, I just wanted you to hear it from me before you put the television news on later today and saw it, especially since you know how they make this stuff up".

"Is Caleb in trouble? Is he okay?" Tom could hear the desperation in Peter's voice and was quick to allay his fears.

"He's not in trouble, he was just trying to fly under the radar and some paparazzi photographer was in the right place at the wrong time last night, that is all. He's staying at a bed and breakfast out bush, apparently, the lady who runs it has young kids and a sick father, Caleb doesn't want them impacted. He is looking out for them, I think that is a good sign, he's not alone, he's not just in his own head anymore, he has let someone else in, and I think that is a good sign, a positive sign."

Tom finished his call with Peter and went to work. There was a lot he had to accomplish, and it needed to be done as soon as humanly possible. His first call was to the owner of the Beryl Creek caravan park, promising them that Caleb would personally mention them in his next big press conference, which was worth hundreds of thousands of dollars in advertising, if they would manufacture a reason to close their caravan park to all members of the press, effective immediately. Tom highlighted the spirit of community, unashamedly informing them that the family that Caleb was staying with, the Bianchi's, were concerned about their privacy. That did the trick, Tom hearing from a disgruntled reporter that they were being made to move. They were all relocating to Bradford, the next town over, as everywhere else in Beryl Creek was booked out. Next, he called in all the favours he was owed by people in the entertainment industry, and he was owed a lot of favours.

By the time his personal assistant was ready to head home, Tom had successfully brokered deals with the majority of the major news networks, newspapers, and magazines around the country and overseas, promising them everything from exclusive interviews with Caleb, high-end gift baskets, setups between themselves and other high profile celebrities they were hoping to interview, tickets to exclusive and sold-out events, and, as he expected, a large number of I owe yous. In return, Tom was assured that none of the news networks, newspapers, and magazines that he contacted would accept any photographs of Caleb, with or without Gabby and her family, for publication. Any news networks, newspapers, and magazines that did print them would be taken to court by Tom on behalf of Caleb. Tom finished off his day by calling Caleb and letting him know that the issue had been fixed, that he could tell his hosts that they don't need to be concerned with going outside the house anymore, that if Caleb wanted him to, Tom would appear in a local court tomorrow morning and apply for restraining orders. Caleb declined, he trusted Tom, if Tom said the issue was fixed, Caleb knew that the issue was fixed.

Promising to talk tomorrow, Caleb disconnected the call. He made his way slowly upstairs, his chest ached, he idly wondered if he was having a heart attack. It didn't take him very long to pack up his belongings, he hadn't brought much to begin with. He debated about saying goodbye to the girls but decided that Gabby probably wouldn't like that very much. He found Nico and Maria in the kitchen, and thanked them for their hospitality, apologising again for any trouble he might have caused them. Gabby was outside, unpacking the cars, ignoring him.

"Gabby," he touched her arm softly.

"Don't touch me!" She spat out, anger boiling over. "You don't get to touch me."

"Gabby, please, I'm sorry, let me explain." Caleb pleaded.

"You deliberately lied to me. Even when I gave you the opportunity to tell me the truth, you lied. Everything you ever told me was a lie. And worse of all Caleb, you told me just now that you would never have let yourself be photographed with me."

"I know you are mad Gabby, but I didn't mean that the way it sounded. I'm sorry. And not everything was a lie, in Bradford, that was the real me, the things I told you, they were all the truth."

"I don't believe you, Caleb. You used me, plain and simple. I was your way of scratching an itch. Well," she shrugged, "I hope you had fun. Don't you ever contact me or my family again Caleb. I mean it, no phone calls, no emails, nothing. I never want to hear from you or see you for as long as I live, is that clear?"

"Gabby," voice full of anguish, Caleb tried again to get Gabby to listen to him, to see his side of the situation. "I'm sorry, please, tell me how to make this right, tell me how to fix this."

"You can't." Gabby looked at Caleb, he could see the unshed tears in her eyes, the way her cheeks were coloured with embarrassment and anger.

He knew she was right, but that didn't make it any easier for him to watch her turn on her heel and walk away, walk away from him, back into the house. He watched her go, silently begging her to turn around, desperately hoping for a sign that she cared, that it wasn't too late for them. She closed the door without a backwards glance. Caleb felt like he had been sucker-punched. He couldn't breathe. He did what he knew how to do best, he ran. Throwing his bags in the boot of his car, he peeled out of Gabby's driveway and accelerated down the street, not caring what speed he was doing, or if anybody saw him. He screamed out onto the highway, narrowly missing a minibus. It should have been sobering, but Caleb didn't even blink. His head was a bad place to be tonight, and he ran as if demons were chasing him. Two hours later he was pulling into the driveway of The Aurora, too tired to continue on to Sydney, determined to forget all about Gabby and her family, determined to erase all traces of Beryl Creek from his thoughts.

CHAPTER SIXTEEN

Laughing, Caleb turned to look at Sam, his eyes twinkling. "See," he couldn't help teasing the other man, "I knew you would have a good time tonight Sammy."

"I always have a good time with you little brother," Sam ruffled Caleb's perfectly lacquered hair, deliberately squashing the rock star 'ruffled fresh from bed' style that Caleb had spent hours perfecting earlier that night. "But we can't all be irresponsible rockstars now can we, Callie?" Sam used the childhood nickname he knew Caleb detested so much, knowing it would get a rise out of him. "Some of us actually have to work to earn a living!" It was the same banter that always existed between them, the ribbing and poking fun that was laced with the love that comes from being part of a family.

"Work?!" snorted Caleb, "Ha! As if! You're a partner in a law firm Sammy, how much work can you possibly do? Don't you have a staff of people all waiting to jump to your command?" Caleb's raucous laugh mingled with Sam's deep chortle.

"Staff? That's your department brother dear, how many do you have now? Eighteen? Ninete-"

"Watch out!" Caleb's panicked shout interrupts Sam, and he blinks once, surprise etching his features. The unrelenting screech of bare metal tyre rims on bitumen reaches a crescendo before fading into silence, the world turning black, the only sound an incessant ringing.

Caleb sat up, momentarily disorientated. He rubbed his hands over his face, looking around the room he found himself in. He had made it as far as the sofa last night, flipping through mind-numbing television channels while he downed a beer. He must have fallen asleep, the television still on, broadcasting the home shopping channel. He watched for a moment, shaking his head and switching it off in disgust when he realised that he was actually considering buying the eight in one kitchen appliance that they were spruiking. His mobile rang again, he sighed, looking around until he found it, half squashed underneath the sofa. "Hello." He snapped, not bothering to feign politeness. It was five o'clock in the morning for crying out loud, he had just endured a crap night's sleep, so whoever it was that was calling, they had better have a good reason.

"Caleb?" The voice was oddly familiar but strained somehow.

"Yes."

"It's Maria."

"Maria," Caleb's thoughts flew in all directions, Gabby, Lucia, Sofia. He was already standing up, reaching for his car keys. "What's wrong?"

"It's Nico, he's in the hospital, the doctors think he had a heart attack. It's bad Caleb, they want to send him to Sydney." Maria ended on a sob, unable to fathom the very real possibility of losing her husband of nearly forty years.

"Which hospital is he in?" Caleb shut the hotel door and crossed to the elevator, impatiently pushing the down button repeatedly, even though he knew, subconsciously, it wouldn't make the elevator appear on his floor any quicker.

"Bradford. He is in the intensive care unit. I just…I thought you would want to know."

"Maria, thank you. I'm on my way, I will be there in five minutes okay?" Caleb disconnected the call, sticking his phone in his pocket as he made his way down to the parking garage.

He hadn't thought much beyond getting to the hospital to be with Gabby, but as he slid into the driver's seat, he wished that he had taken the time to shower and change, to grab a cup of coffee and to formulate some kind of plan. He was starting to have second thoughts, sneaky little doubts were creeping in. He had no idea if Gabby knew that he was on his way, or if she did, if she even cared one way or the other. He was desperate to see her, even though he knew it would end up with her hating him even more than she most likely already did. He needed to see her, to hank her. She stopped his nightmares, he didn't have any at all the night that they had spent together, not that it mattered, there wasn't about to be a repeat, no, he would just have to get used to dealing with them again, that was all. He scrolled through his navigational system until he found the local hospital, adding it in and then choosing directions. Caleb pulled out of the parking garage slowly, half expecting to be swarmed by paparazzi, but found no one lying in wait for him, which was a relief, given his current bad mood, he didn't trust himself not to run them down on purpose.

He easily found a parking space at the hospital, which was bigger than he imagined that it would be and slipped on his sunglasses. He took the first available elevator up to the second floor, following the signs for the intensive care unit. He found Maria pacing outside the closed ward, Lucia and Sofia sitting quietly on the hard plastic chairs.

"Maria?"

"Caleb," she embraced him firmly, kissing his cheeks distractedly.

"How is he? Is there any news?" Caleb guided Maria over to the seats, gently pushing her down on to one next to Lucia and Sofia.

"No, no one has come out yet. I have been sitting with the girls while Gabby spends some time with her father," Maria looks at Caleb sideways, "she, ah, doesn't know that I called you."

"Maria," Caleb groaned aloud, "you should not have done that, Gabby will not be very happy with you at all."

"When is she ever?" Maria brushed Caleb's concern aside. "I made a lot of mistakes as a mother Caleb, and as a grandmother," Maria's voice catches in her throat, "I thought I was doing what was best, I thought I knew best, better than Gabby, better than Nico. It is my fault he is here; it is my fault he is sick." A sob breaks free from Maria, and she hastily rummages through her handbag in search of a tissue.

"Maria," Caleb sits next to the older woman and slings his arms over her shoulders. "There is no way that any of this is your fault Maria, no way at all." Of this Caleb is certain.

"It is," she dabs her eyes with the balled-up tissue. "After you left last night, Nico tried talking to Gabby, tried to find out what had happened between the two of you," she blushed slightly, "I mean, not the intimate stuff, of course, but…The other stuff, the personal stuff. She wouldn't talk to him, she just tidied up after dinner and then went into the office to finish up some work." Maria shook her head sadly and dabbed at her eyes.

"I thought she was being petty, Nico told me not to interfere, but I wouldn't listen. I went to talk to her. We got into a fight; it was pretty bad. Actually, that isn't true, it was honest."

"An honest fight?"

"Yes. Caleb, she wouldn't tell me what had happened between the two of you, not all of it in any case, but she did tell me about your brother, I am so sorry, I can only imagine how you must feel…" Maria trailed off, touching Caleb's cheek the way a mother would. "Gabby also had some other home truths for me. About the way I have treated her as opposed to her sister, about the way Lucia and Sofia came to her. She wasn't very kind to me last night, I realise now that I deserved it of course, but last night I wasn't ready to listen, so we did what we always do, we argued."

"I can imagine." After hearing how Gabby felt about her mother's interference and favouritism towards her younger sister, Caleb was only surprised by how long it had actually taken her to stand up for herself.

"Nico heard us, I feel so embarrassed, the whole street must have heard us sniping at each other." If Maria hadn't been so serious Caleb would have found the whole thing rather funny. "Nico tried to intervene, tried to placate us both, but as much as Gabby might wish that she was nothing like me, it was my temper that she inherited, not his fair nature. So, he tried to reason with us, and it escalated into the three of us all arguing at once, a little triangle of anger. And then," Maria draws a deep, shaking breath, "Nico just collapsed, he just slumped sideways in his chair and then he turned grey and just fell to the floor." She was sobbing again now, Lucia and Sofia snuggling closer to each other, eyes wide. "It is all my fault, if I had just listened to Nico, if I had just held off on talking with Gabby, this wouldn't have happened, Nico wouldn't have gotten so worked up that he collapsed."

"Maria, I am sure the doctors will tell you the same thing, but I doubt very much if it was this incident alone that triggered Nico's collapse. Maybe there is an underlying issue?"

"Maybe, I don't know. I just…I thought…Nico likes you, we both do, it is only right that you be here."

"Maria, let me sit with the girls, you go back to Nico. We'll be okay, we'll go get some food at the cafeteria or something, you can call me if you get worried or you need anything, and we will be right back."

"Thank you, I really would like to go back to him, I want to see him."

"Of course, go, we'll be fine, won't we Lucia and Sofia?" The two little girls nodded enthusiastically, Caleb was fun, maybe he would take them for ice cream if they asked nicely. They hugged Maria goodbye, Lucia and Sofia taking Caleb's hands and happily following the coloured line marker down to the cafeteria. They ordered one of everything, way too much food, but Caleb knew a picnic would distract everyone, and went to find a shady spot on the lawns to sit.

It wasn't long before an angry-looking Gabby slammed through the kiosk doors, uncaring of who was around to witness her mood. "Lucia, Sofia, pick up your things and come with me please, now!" The girls hastened to obey, they knew what mama's angry tone sounded like and no way did they want to get into trouble.

"Hello, Gabby. Why, hello Caleb." Caleb suggested quietly, earning a look of absolute fury from Gabby. Honestly, if fire were to come spitting from her eyes right now, he would not be at all surprised.

"Are you actually trying to talk to me right now?" Her rebuttal was scathing. Caleb was beginning to wish that he had let her loose on the paparazzi, now that would have been a sight to see.

"Gabby, come on," he tried again, "why don't you sit down for a minute, have something to eat, I know you must be hungry."

"You don't know anything Caleb." She took Lucia and Sofia's hands in her own and turned back towards the banks of elevators.

Caleb hastened to collect up all the food, shoving it back into the bag and jogging after the girls. "If you are not going to sit and eat with me, then at least take the food back with you." Caleb held the bag out towards Gabby, who resolutely ignored it. "If you don't want it, that's fine. At least take it for Maria and the girls, Gabby, don't be so stubborn. You know as well as I do that everyone is hungry, this will save you all a trip to the store later, I know Maria doesn't want to have to leave Nico's side right now." Caleb wasn't above a little blackmail if it meant that she would eat something, she looked dead on her feet. With gritted teeth and lips pressed in an uncompromising line, Gabby held her hand out for the bag of food, flinching slightly when Caleb passed it over, deliberately letting his fingers linger on hers for a moment too long. Where was this darn elevator?! Gabby tapped her foot impatiently, wondering just when Caleb was going to get the message and go away. As she and the girls stood in the elevator watching the doors close, Gabby sighed in relief, a relief that was short-lived when she exited at the top level to see Caleb standing there, not even sweating from what must a been a herculean run up the stairs.

CHAPTER SEVENTEEN

Gabby allowed the girls to walk ahead to their nanna, carrying the bag of food between them. As they turned the corner into the intensive care waiting room, Gabby rounded on Caleb. "You can leave now." She reminded him curtly.

"Gabby, let me help you, let me help your family."

"We don't need your help, Caleb," Gabby hissed seething, "and even if we did, we wouldn't want it, nor would we even accept it."

"Your mother already did." He reminded her flatly.

"A mistake she won't make again, especially not with my daughters."

"Gabby, please, let me help you. Let me pay off the debts at the bakery, let me hire you some help, a housekeeper to help your mum with the bed and breakfast, some staff for the bakery so you have more time at home, I know you want these things Gabby, let me give them to you, it is the least that I can do."

"The least that you can do? For what exactly Caleb? For lying to me?"

"Gabby, that's not why. You have no idea how much it helped me, to talk to you about Sam that night we had together. I haven't talked about him before, not with anyone."

"So, what you are actually saying then Caleb is that you are essentially paying me because I listened? Or maybe it is payment for services rendered?"

"Gabby, no! that is not how it was, not for me and not for you, I know that you know that. Don't pretend that it was anything less than what it was, don't brush off what we have just because you are angry with me."

"What we have Caleb? No, what we had, which, by the way, was a one-night stand, nothing more than that. you could have had that with anyone, I was simply convenient, an easy target."

"Gabby, no, it wasn't like that. I, I know it sounds completely insane, especially coming from me now, when I should have said it earlier, but it was more than a one-night stand Gabby." Caleb took a deep breath before continuing. "I love you." He knew that she would have a strong reaction, but the sharp sting of her palm connecting with the side of his face was not what he had imagined would happen.

"Don't ever say that again," Gabby fumed. "I do not want to hear it, is that clear? I hate you, Caleb, do you understand that, I hate you."

"Gabby," Caleb's voice is strangled, "don't say that, please don't say that."

"Why not Caleb, it is the truth." Gabby shrugged her shoulders, determined to act as if she really did not care.

"Gabby, please."

"You lied to me, consistently and on purpose. You pretended to enjoy spending time with me and my family, all while living a secret life. You all but admitted that you did not want to be seen in public with me, I realise now that it was so there would be no photos of the famous Caleb Roman slumming it with some small-town single mum, a pleb baker of all things. God, how you must have mocked us, how you must have laughed at our small ways. Was it some kind of joke

Caleb? Are you planning on writing a song about this, your foray into the real world, your brush with the commoner?"

"Gabby, I would never, you have my word."

"Oh good, since that is so trustworthy," she mocked. "Do you think I am stupid Caleb? I can't trust you. Just go home, go back where you belong, you aren't wanted here." With that Gabby turned on her heel, stalking down the empty corridor and around the corner.

Once out of Caleb's sight, Gabby sunk into the nearest plastic chair she saw, hands shaking, unable to catch her breath properly. God how she hated that man! She shook her head firmly, trying to clear her foggy thoughts. No, she didn't hate him, not really, not even close, but she wanted to, with every fibre of her being she wanted to hate him for the rest of her life. The only problem was, deep down she knew that he had not done anything wrong, not really. Oh, sure, he had lied to them all, but it wasn't maliciously done, of that she was certain. It was done from a place of self-preservation. No, the problem wasn't with Caleb, it was with her. He had made her feel alive, electric, vibrant. Which was the real problem, because now that Gabby knew who Caleb really was, there was no way that they could ever be together. He was way out of her league; he was so far out of her league he was in a different solar system. Gabby wasn't an idiot, it didn't matter how much he liked her or her family, the fact remained that they were from different walks of life.

She came from the working class, she knew where she would be in ten years' time, she would still be in her parent's bakery, running it for them. She would head home in the evenings and cook for them, tidying up the house before bed. The girls would be away at university, no matter what it took,

Gabby was going to make sure that both Lucia and Sofia went to university, that they had the opportunity she never had. No way would they work in the bakery. This was her lot in life, it would not be theirs. This is who she was, this is what she had in store for her. Caleb only served to remind her of that. He was the first thing she had done for herself; he had reminded her of all the things she had once yearned for, and now he was the reason she would never have any of it. Caleb had been right, it had been more than a one-night stand, she had gone ahead and stupidly fallen in love with him. She could never have him, but she knew she would torture herself by reading all about him in the tabloids, watching him live out his life carefree. She knew that while she couldn't have him, she also would never settle for anything less. She had doomed herself for one night with Caleb, a mistake she would never forgive herself for.

CHAPTER EIGHTEEN

Caleb threw the car into reverse and peeled out of the hospital parking garage, headed back to the seclusion and silence of his hotel room, needing to get as far away from Gabby as quickly as he could. He couldn't hear anything over the rushing of the blood in his ears, she couldn't really hate him, could she? He knew that he needed to make this right, he just needed to formulate a plan first. Once he was holed up in his room, he poured himself a large scotch and, rifling around in the small desk in the corner, located a piece of paper and a pen, sitting down at the table and beginning to write. Two hours later he was finished, he leant back in his chair and flexed his fingers, trying to dispel the cramps that had taken up residence an hour ago. Caleb wasn't used to writing by hand, he usually just scribbled some notes down and left the actual writing work for when he was sitting in front of his laptop. He fingered the list he had just made, right now it seemed insurmountable, but he had no other options, he knew what he had to do if he ever hoped to prove to Gabby that she mattered to him, that she wasn't just someone that he had used for his own pleasure, his own end, he just wished that it wasn't going to be so hard.

Caleb stood and walked across the room to the sliding glass door of the balcony, opening it and slipping outside. It had grown dark outside while he had written, the coolness of the air surprised him. The town below was bathed in the glow of streetlights, with no lights on inside the hotel room, he was clothed in darkness. He leant on the railing, watched a young couple laugh as they walked down the street, he wondered where they were going at this hour, twilight. A dog barked his disapproval, his owner attempting to rush him past a tree before he was able to lift his leg. Caleb wondered who was watching Bella and Jellybean, he knew Lucia and Sofia must be missing them something fierce. With a sigh, he sunk down onto one of the sun lounges on the balcony. He knew he was stalling, trying to put off the task at hand. A vision of Gabby flashed in his head, she was standing before him, floral sundress wafting in the breeze, brilliant smile directed at him. She was dazzling, and she was worth it.

Caleb picked up his mobile phone and dialled a familiar number, waiting for it to connect at the other end.

"Hello?" The voice sounded tired, Caleb silently cursed himself, he should have checked the time first, they were probably just about to sit down for an evening in front of the television, bingeing their favourite television show.

"Mum?" Hope mingled with regret; he didn't know what he would do if she hung up on him.

"Caleb," she gasped, Caleb imagined her standing at the phone clutching her chest. "Oh my god, is it really you?" Caleb could hear her crying softly.

"Yes, mum, it is me. I just wanted to let you know that I am coming home, back to Sydney. I have a few things that I want to take care of."

"Really? You're coming home?"

"Yes mum, I'm coming home."

"When?"

"I'm going to leave first thing in the morning, I should be back home by tomorrow afternoon, early evening at the latest.

Why don't you and dad come over tomorrow night for dinner, we'll order in from that Irish place you like so much."

"Really?" He hated the hesitant eagerness in her voice. Had he really been that horrid to her, chased her away that much that she now questioned her place in his life? "You want us to come over tomorrow for dinner?"

"Yes mum, I do. We can talk about Sam's memorial; I can tell you my plans."

"Caleb, we don't have to."

"I want to talk about him mum, I am ready to talk about him." Caleb remained firm.

"Okay then Caleb, we will see you tomorrow evening. Caleb?" Judy called out just before Caleb hung up the phone.

"Yes, mum."

"I love you."

"I love you too mum." He disconnected the call, feeling lighter than he had in months. Everything would be okay, or it wouldn't, but either way, he was not going to go down without a fight, that was for certain. Returning back inside, Caleb left his mobile phone on the coffee table, using the room phone to call down to the reception and request a wake-up call for the following morning, and then, fully clothed, he flopped across the king-sized bed, feet dangling off the edge, and drifted off to sleep.

Laughing, Caleb turned to look at Sam, his eyes twinkling. "See," he couldn't help teasing the other man, "I knew you would have a good time tonight Sammy."

"I always have a good time with you little brother," Sam ruffled Caleb's perfectly lacquered hair, deliberately squashing the rock star 'ruffled fresh from bed' style that Caleb had spent hours perfecting earlier that night. "But we can't all be irresponsible rockstars now can we, Callie?" Sam used the childhood nickname he knew Caleb detested so much, knowing it would get a rise out of him. "Some of us actually have to work to earn a living!" It was the same banter that always existed between them, the ribbing and poking fun that was laced with the love that comes from being part of a family.

"Work?!" snorted Caleb, "Ha! As if! You're a partner in a law firm Sammy, how much work can you possibly do? Don't you have a staff of people all waiting to jump to your command?" Caleb's raucous laugh mingled with Sam's deep chortle.

"Staff? That's your department brother dear, how many do you have now? Eighteen? Ninete-"

"Watch out!" Caleb's panicked shout interrupts Sam, and he blinks once, surprise etching his features. The unrelenting screech of bare metal tyre rims on bitumen reaches a crescendo before fading into silence, the world turning black, the only sound an incessant beep, beep, beep.

It took Caleb a minute to realise that the beeping was his mobile phone, and another minute to pad out to the lounge room to retrieve it off the coffee table. He checked his text messages quickly, a couple from his parents wondering if he had gotten away okay, one from his agent double checking if Caleb was sure he wanted to do the morning shows, and one from Gabby. Caleb's heart skipped a beat as he opened it with trembling fingers.

They are transferring dad to the St Vincent's Hospital in Sydney, mum said you would want to know.

Good, St Vincent's was the best in Sydney for cardiac patients, and it had the added benefit of only being twelve minutes from Caleb's house. Caleb sent a quick text back to his parents, letting them know he was heading out the door now, one to his agent saying an emphatic yes, and then one to Gabby, letting her know he was grateful she had told him, and that he would be thinking of them all. He waited a few moments, but there was no reply.

With a resigned sigh, Caleb showered, dressed, checked out and was pulling out of the parking garage before it was even time for the receptionist to call him with his wake-up call. Caleb loved this time of the morning when the world around him was still waking up. He swung into the drive-thru of a popular fast-food chain to grab a coffee, treated himself to a chocolate iced doughnut with sprinkles on top, and then re-joined the traffic, slipping in behind a semi-trailer, content to just relax and take his time in getting home, not in any hurry. As Caleb sipped at his coffee and chewed on his sticky doughnut, he let his mind wander. It was a curious thing, he thought, to realise that he was not at all anxious about returning home. Even after all of his nightmares, after his guilt and pushing others away, he was oddly calm about going home. He was ready now, ready to face up to Sam's death, to say goodbye and to move on.

His parents were already waiting when Caleb pulled into the driveway of his Sydney house, he could see the worry etched on to their faces, and was quick to reassure them that everything was okay. "Mum, Dad, I got stuck in traffic."

"Caleb," his mother pulled him into a tight hug, tears misting her eyes. "I missed you so much, I am so glad that you are home."

"Me too mum," he squeezed her back. He had missed this sense of family, missed his mother's warm embraces and his father's quiet looks. "Come on, I'm starving, let's get some food." He laughed, lightening the mood. As promised, Caleb ordered from his mother's favourite place, O'Malley's restaurant, the trio feasting on baked potatoes loaded with toppings, hearty lamb stew, and fresh crusty bread rolls. They spoke of mundane things, of safe topics, while they ate. They discussed the weather, his need for a haircut, what his parents were planting in their garden this year. All the while Sam was at the back of Caleb's mind, patiently waiting.

"Would you like some dessert mum?" Caleb offered, knowing his mother's sweet tooth.

"What do you have?"

"Actually, I'm not sure," he crossed the room into the kitchen, opening the freezer and peering in. "Chocolate ice cream, fruit tarts, chocolate brownies…" he trailed off, waiting for an answer.

"I'll have a small bowl of ice cream please." Caleb fished out the container of ice cream, carrying it to the bench. Opening it, he stared, bursting into laughter. "Caleb, what's so funny?"

"Sorry mum, no ice cream after all," Caleb held up the container, full of a jar of whipping cream and three ice cubes, "just another one of Sam's practical jokes." He saw the worried glance that passed between his parents, his laughter dying.

"What? It is okay to talk about him, we need, I need, to talk about him. I'll surely go crazy if I don't."

"Caleb," it was his father's worried warning that left him breathless.

"What?" Caleb snarled. "Now we can't talk about him? You wanted me to talk about him for weeks, you wouldn't shut up about it! Now suddenly you don't want me to. What is it? Am I only allowed to talk about Sam when it suits you?" Caleb knew he was being unfair, but he couldn't stop himself, it was as if a dam had burst inside of him. "He was my brother, mine! Do you think that I didn't see, didn't know, that you loved him more than me? Do you think I don't know that you wished it was me who had died instead of Sam? Do you think that I don't wish that too? Sam was eminently more than I was, than I am, than I ever will be. I know that. you were right, it should have been me, not Sam, who had died that night."

"Caleb, we never thought that, never, we-" His mother tried to placate him.

"Don't lie to me," Caleb's voice was anguished. "I heard you say it, I heard you say that it should have been me that had died, not Sam."

"What?" His father was confused, his mother openly weeping now, distress clouding her features. "We never said…" Caleb's dad trailed off. "Caleb, when was this?"

"In the hospital," Caleb replied flatly. "I don't blame you for saying that, you only said what everyone else was thinking anyway."

"Caleb, that isn't what we said," his father started. "I mean, those were the words I spoke, but the context was very different. You see," his father moved closer to Caleb, "your mother hadn't left your side, the doctors came to see us, but she refused to leave you, so I went instead. What you heard was me relaying the doctor's message to your mother. They had told me that you should have died in that crash Caleb, not Sam. Based on your positions in the car, it should have been you that we all lost. Sam gave his life to save yours, Caleb, he threw his body across yours moments before the crash, he saved your life, Caleb, at the cost of his. His death was not in vain, and it was not your fault. He died for love Caleb, and while we never wanted to ever have to lose any of our children before us, the way that he died, selflessly protecting the brother that he adored, well," his dad cleared his throat, "that gives us great comfort."

CHAPTER NINETEEN

Caleb didn't know what to say. He could hear sobs wrenching, echoing in his ears. Were they his? His mother's? He wasn't sure. His head was spinning, was it true? He couldn't remember much from the crash, the doctors had said that it was perfectly normal, that he may never remember everything that had happened, a combination of the concussion and the sneaky way in which a brain tried to protect a person from the full knowledge of what had happened. An in-built protection system. "Why? Why would he do that?" Caleb's voice sounded far away, even to his own ears. "Why would he give up his own life, to save me? Why? He was a lawyer for crying out loud, he made a difference, he had his whole life ahead of him, why would he do such a stupid thing?"

"Caleb, don't you dare!" His mother was shouting now, really shouting. "You make people happy Caleb, your music does that, it brings people together. There is no comparison, don't even try, there is no difference to how important Sam was to how important you are, no difference at all, you both made a difference to people, you just did it in different ways, and Sam knew that".

"He didn't need to die," Caleb spoke more to himself than to anybody else.

"No," his mother whispered hoarsely, "but he did, and we just have to try our best to go on without him here with us."

"I miss him, I miss him so much, I just want him back here with me." Caleb sobbed.

"I know you do, we all do." Caleb's mother embraced him, holding her youngest tightly in her arms, his father coming up behind them and wrapping his arms around them both. Caleb wasn't sure how long they stayed there like this, the three of them holding each other and crying, and he didn't care. It was a release, it was as if a valve had been shut off inside of Caleb for far too long, tonight's dinner had opened it, allowed the contents to stream out. He knew that he would always miss Sam, would always wish that he was here with him, but tonight had helped him to feel lighter, to feel a little more settled within himself. He hadn't killed his brother, after all, it had not been his fault that Sam had died. Sam had died willingly, instinctively, in order to protect Caleb. Sam had given his final breath to his family, a thought that sobered Caleb and made him determined to live regret-free.

Once their tears had subsided, Caleb's mother busied herself with making coffee, bringing it through to the open plan lounge room to join her husband and son once it was ready. Over coffee, Caleb told his parents how he had struggled with Sam's death, apologising for shutting them out for so long, he regretted that now, he wondered if it would have been easier to cope with losing Sam had he known that Sam had sacrificed himself in order to save Caleb? Caleb told his parents about his visit to Beryl Creek, leaving nothing but the finer details out. He wanted to be honest with them, he didn't want any secrets from his parents, not anymore.

"Do you love her?" Caleb's father asked him once he had finished telling him all about Gabby.

"Yes." Caleb didn't hesitate, sadness colouring his voice. He wasn't sure when he had fallen in love with Gabby, but he had. "But it is too late dad, she hates me."

"Well then, what are you going to do to win her back?"

"I don't know what else I can do dad, I already offered to buy the bakery from her, to hire her some staff for around the house, until her father recovers, she threw it back in my face."

"Hmm," Caleb's mum said dryly, "I wonder why. Honestly Caleb," she shook her head, "do you hear yourself? You offered her money, that is all. If I were in her position, I would tell you to get lost as well, seriously, think about how that sounds Caleb, you took her to bed and then you offered her financial compensation. No wonder she said no, you have a lot to learn about women son."

"I have been such an idiot," Caleb lamented miserably. "I didn't think about it like that, how on earth am I ever going to be able to fix this mess?"

"If she loves you, she will forgive you, just don't do anything tonight okay?" Caleb's dad cautioned.

"Why not?"

"Caleb, it is two o'clock in the morning, no one is that forgiving!"

Caleb's parents agreed to stay the night, Caleb had more than enough spare bedrooms, and they didn't relish the thought of driving across the city at this hour of the night. Once in his room, Caleb lay on his bed, staring at the ceiling. He knew he had to win Gabby back, and he knew how he had to do it, but his plan was a huge gamble, if it failed and she refused him again, he wasn't quite sure what he would do then. Caleb was determined to leave his past in the past where it belonged, and not bring it into his future, he only hoped Gabby would be able to see that, that she still trusted him enough to listen to him. Having formulated a plan, Caleb found it hard to drift off to sleep, he was restless, he wanted to be moving, putting his plan into action, not twiddling his thumbs waiting until morning. Knowing his father was right, that he should not contact Gabby at this hour, he settled for the next best thing, calling St Vincent's Hospital and asking after her father. Caleb was reassured after his telephone call, Gabby's father had undergone surgery, and although he was in a serious condition, he was expected to make a full recovery. Logging in to his laptop, Caleb brought up the website for a well-known florist and ordered a large bunch of bright flowers to be delivered to Nico in the morning. That done, Caleb settled down for the night, slipping off into a dreamless sleep.

CHAPTER TWENTY

Caleb all but bounced out of bed the following morning, eager to get started on making amends with Gabby. He took his parents out for a leisurely breakfast at a nearby café, happily agreeing to pose for a couple of photographs with fans as he was heading into the café, no doubt making their day. He received a stilted text message from Gabby halfway through breakfast, thanking him for the flowers on behalf of her mother who had thought them beautiful and spent the rest of the meal with a lovesick grin on his face. His parents made him promise to text them as soon as he got home, Caleb now realising that his parents would no doubt be nervous about saying goodbye to their children every single time from now on. The drive across Sydney was backed up bumper to bumper, a by-product of roadworks according to the local radio news network Caleb tuned in to.

He pulled into Tom's office building, a sleek high rise, catering to only the very elite, there were no signs on the building, if you knew the address, you were in a different class of people. Caleb boycotted the elevator in favour of the stairs, easily jogging up the three flights to his agent's floor. He didn't have an appointment, had never needed one, a smile and a wink at the receptionist usually did the trick, although now that Caleb thought about it, that seemed like something he shouldn't be doing anymore, not if he wanted Gabby to keep talking to him at any rate. He needn't have worried, as he exited the stairs into the foyer, Tom was already there waiting for him.

"Psychic, now are we?" He joked by way of a greeting.

"Your mum called me." Tom embraced his friend warmly, it was good to see him back in town, and just as good to see him looking happy.

"I see you got a bit of a head start this morning if those fans gushing to the local television network are anything to go by." Tom gently chided his friend.

"Why not," Caleb shrugged, "it feels good to give back. Speaking of which, I want you to book me on Breakfast With Bernie."

"I'm sorry, what?" Tom opened his office door, motioning for Caleb to go on in ahead of him. "You cook now?" Tom could not have been more surprised than if Caleb had asked him to book him for dental surgery, so famous was Caleb for being unable to cook anything.

"Kind of," Caleb confessed sheepishly, "it is a long story, just do it for me, please?"

"Does this have something to do with Gabby?"

"Seriously? How do you know about that?"

"Your mum."

"You two are worse than a pair of old women, gossiping over the fence." Caleb sighed, then told his friend his plan, wanting to confide in someone rather than seeking approval for it.

Caleb spent the entire day holed up with Tom, along with Nate, drummer of the Three Odd Lizards, and Alex, lead vocals of the Three Odd Lizards. Caleb, Nate, and Alex had been best friends since high school, connecting through a love of music and a desire to flout the rules. While the latter had changed, the former had not, and the three friends greeted each other as if they had only parted hours before, picking up their conversation as if one of them had merely returned from the bathroom instead of a twelve-month self-imposed hiatus. There were no questions asked, instead, the three friends embraced each other warmly, accepting, forgiving, and then sat down and got back to work. The day was spent going over the schedule for the following few days, it was one of the busiest schedules the Three Odd Lizards had needed to adhere to in recent years, but it was time. Tom was in complete agreeance, it was time the world was put on notice, Caleb and the Three Odd Lizards were back.

By the time Caleb finally returned home that evening, it was close to midnight. He shot a quick text message off to his father, internally debated about sending one to Gabby or not, but ultimately decided not to, instead, opting for a long swim in the pool before heading to bed. The next few days were going to be brutal, Caleb and the Three Odd Lizards were booked to do a series of interviews with the local television networks, including several of the morning shows, as well as a couple of game shows and a cooking show. On top of which, there were magazine interviews and photoshoots, a couple of charity events, and Caleb still needed to convince Gabby that he loved her and that she really ought to stop being so stubborn and just agree to marry him. It was while he was mentally designing Gabby's wedding ring that Caleb finally fell asleep.

CHAPTER TWENTY-ONE

The television studio lights were way too bright, Caleb was already sweating, and they had yet to ask him any questions. The producers had obviously decided to go with the young, beautiful interviewer, Caleb noted wryly. The irony wasn't lost on him, hell, eighteen months ago he would have flirted with her throughout the entire interview, before ushering her to her dressing room backstage during the commercial break. Surprisingly, he wasn't the least bit wistful of those days. Alex and Nate sat on either side of Caleb, flanking him. Caleb knew that they were on Tom's orders to step in should anyone have the audacity to dare enquire about Sam. Caleb knew that his parents would be watching, they always did, and he hoped that Gabby and Maria would be as well.

The interview started off generically enough, there were the standard questions relating to the Three Odd Lizards touring schedule and the exciting new music that they had been working on, before the interviewer graced Caleb with an over the top sweetness smile and stated "Now tell me, Caleb, I heard that you got yourself stranded in Berry Creek," she shuddered, "I cannot even imagine how that must have been for you, please, tell everyone tuning in today, however did you survive it?"

"It was Beryl Creek, Natasha," Caleb ignored her ill attempts at flirting, and instead shot the television camera one of his sexiest smiles, "and to be honest with you all, it was a little slice of paradise. They have the best bakery that I have ever been into, seriously, the cakes and pastries that they sell, mmmm hmmmmm," Caleb smacked his lips together in anticipation, "utterly divine, and completely sinful." He shot the audience a wink.

At this point Caleb had the live audience eating out of his hands, they giggled and oohed and aahed with him.

"My my, did you spend all of your time at this bakery?" Natasha sniped.

"More or less," Caleb shrugged, not bothering to elaborate. "The bakery is owned by an Italian family, the Bianchi's. If anyone is up that way, stop in and tell them I said hello, they will treat you right, you won't be sorry, I promise." The interview moved on to other things, Caleb was happy to let Alex and Nate field questions, his job done. He had put his plan into action, he had put the Bianchi's bakery on the map. It was a mantra he repeated throughout the day, with each new interview he gave a new plug. By the end of the day, he had spoken about the Bianchi bakery to eight television reporters, sixteen magazine reporters, nine newspaper reporters, and one starstruck television cooking show host. Not bad for a day's work.

On the way home from the last interview of the day, Caleb found himself subconsciously taking a detour, finding himself pulling up in front of St Vincent's Hospital. He was desperate to go in, to see everyone again, but he didn't dare, not now that he was back in circulation, not when there was a chance of a reporter seeing him and digging up a story. Instead, he sat in his car and dialled Maria's mobile phone number, waiting for her to answer.

"Hello."

"Maria? It's Caleb."

"Caleb," she chirped, sounding absolutely delighted to be hearing from him. Caleb smiled in spite of himself. "How are you? I saw you on one of those morning shows today, you looked very dashing, are those other two men in your band as well?"

"Alex and Nate, they sure are, the three of us make up the band, although we do occasionally make use of backup singers. They also happen to be my best friends." Caleb wasn't sure why he added the last bit, for some reason he was feeling nervous.

"Well, we all thought that you were very fine this morning Caleb, you looked content." All? Did she mean…Was Gabby and the girls in Sydney too?

"How is…Everyone?" He asked lamely, all the while screaming in his head, Gabby, tell me about Gabby.

"She isn't here Caleb," Maria saw right through his ruse. He tried not to let it bother him, but he was disappointed. He had hoped to be able to see her, in person. "She and the girls had to go back to Beryl Creek, Lucia and Sofia have school, and we weren't sure how long Nico would need to stay in hospital. And then there was the bakery…" Maria trailed off.

"I see, of course, it makes sense. Is, ah, something wrong with the bakery?"

"Caleb," Maria laughed, such a carefree sound it took Caleb by surprise. "There is nothing wrong with the bakery at all. Gabby called me about an hour after your first television interview, she had just gone to open up for the day, and there was already a queue! Caleb, seriously, you didn't have to do that, you didn't have to tell everyone that you had been."

"I'm sorry Maria, do you mind terribly?"

"Caleb, no! I think it is one of the sweetest things anyone has ever done for us, for Gabby," she spoke her daughter's name softly, "but I know it must have cost you. You won't have any privacy in Beryl Creek again, not from the tourists at least, if you decide to come back."

"I would like to," Caleb confessed.
"I know you would." Maria agreed.
"I love her," Caleb whispered.
"I know you do." Maria was not at all surprised by Caleb's confession, she knew love when she saw it, and going on television, when you were as famous as Maria now knew that Caleb was, when you craved your privacy to mourn in, as Maria knew Caleb did, well, that was saying something. You didn't do something like that out of pity or guilt, no, that could only be done from a place of deep love.
"She hates me." Caleb moaned miserably.
"She loves you." Maria countered.
"What?" Caleb was speechless.

"Trust me, Caleb, a mother knows. She had her pride wounded Caleb, but deep down I know she loves you; she just needs time." Caleb hoped that Maria was right, about Gabby loving him in any case, he was less enthused about the time issue. Caleb was not known for being patient, once he made a decision, that was usually it, it generally happened immediately. "Michael hurt her immensely, and then, I wasn't very kind," Maria cleared her throat, "I, well, no doubt you know how things were, I know she opened up to you, that was a big step for her, to put herself first, to trust you."
"I will make this right Maria, I swear it."
"We know you will," she paused, "Nico and I are going home on Monday, oh, he will still be in the hospital of course,

for a few weeks at least, but after that, well, doctors think he will be as good as new."

"Maria, that is wonderful news!"

"He might even regain the use of his legs Caleb if you believe that. They don't have much in the way of physiotherapy in Beryl Creek, but while we have been here, the doctors did scans on his spine and found a small piece of scar tissue. They will try to laser it off tomorrow, he won't even be under an anaesthetic, he will just be sitting there. I would never have imagined."

"Do you need anything Maria? Do you want me to come and sit with you?" Caleb wasn't sure how he would manage that with all the media attention, but if she asked him to, he would find a way.

"No, thank you. We have some friends from Sydney that we kept in touch with after we moved, they have been a wonderful support to us both, a real blessing, to know that people still care even after you wrote them off, isn't it Caleb?" Thinking of his parents, of Alex and Nate, Caleb had to agree that it was, indeed, a blessing.

When Caleb returned home, he could not settle down, he was restless. He wandered around the house, looking for something to do, gravitating towards the music room. He opened the door slowly, bathing the room in light. Everything was exactly where he had left it, untouched and pristine. He ran his hand gently over the keys of his piano, perfectly tuned, there was music to be made here, he knew it. He crossed the room to his guitar stands, his collection was much larger than space here allowed for, but he made sure he kept his favourite guitars here, seventeen in total. They fairly shone under his gaze, a range of acoustic and electric numbers, in a variety of finishes. He selected a deep velvet blue acoustic, sitting in a discarded beanbag, his favourite place to sit and strum. He found the notes easily, memory a wonderful thing, a riff forming in his mind. As it took shape, Caleb jumped up and dashed off, rifling through a drawer until he found what he was looking for, producing a pen and paper and returning to his perch to start composing. He felt energized, empowered, as the music flowed through him, and it wasn't until dawn streaked the sky that he finally laid his guitar down and headed off to bed.

CHAPTER TWENTY-TWO

Caleb woke with a heavy heart, he had been back in Sydney for a little over a week now, and up until this point had managed to keep busy. Between doing band interviews, catching up with his parents, his regular late-night phone calls with Maria, and his current obsessive songwriting all through the nights, he had almost forgotten what day it was. Almost. He rubbed his hand over his eyes in an effort to dislodge the memories buried there, but to no avail. His parents were meeting him here, they were going to drive over to the chapel together. Caleb wondered if it was because they were worried that he might leave town again, not that he would, not this time. He knew he had to face this, he had to say his goodbye, he had to accept what had happened, and why it had happened, or he would never be right within himself again, and if he wasn't okay within his soul, he would never be good enough for Gabby and the girls.

He made his way slowly through to the bathroom, showering and dressing in his sombre black suit. His suit was tailor-made, and Caleb knew that Sam had loved seeing his baby brother act all grown up. It was fitting that Caleb wear this suit today, Sam had been with Caleb the day he had ordered this. They had gone together, had made a day of it, lunching, and hanging out. Sam had loved this suit on Caleb, the memory of it made Caleb smile. Caleb forwent breakfast in favour of a strong black coffee, taking it out onto the front patio to await the arrival of his parents. They were on time, the drive to the chapel silent, each of them lost in their own thoughts. Caleb wasn't at all surprised to see the chapel so full it was overflowing with people, mourners spilling out of the chapel and on to the adjoining botanical gardens, one of Sam's favourite places and the reason that they had chosen this as the location in which to honour his memory and to celebrate his life.

Despite Tom's best efforts, Caleb knew that there would be at least a few of the nation's less scrupulous magazines and news outlets here today, hoping for a scandalous photograph of the grieving family. Caleb shook his head, he never understood why the media was so intent on shooting themselves in the foot. He had always been very upfront with the media, even before the Three Odd Lizards had reached the stratosphere of stardom, if they respected his privacy and that of his family, then he would happily give them exclusive access to him or opportunities to get a candid photograph or quote, but come after him or his family, and he would have them blacklisted, he would make sure they never had access to him or the Three Odd Lizards for the duration of their careers. This open policy that they had with the media was one of the reasons why the Three Odd Lizards were so well-liked and supported by the majority of the media.

The service was just as Caleb imagined it would be, memories were shared, tears were shed, there were even moments of laughter. Photographs were displayed showing Sam's life from squalling baby and chubby toddler to awkward teenager and college graduate. Sam had always seen the good in every situation, there wasn't a single photograph of him where he was not smiling. Judy and Peter both spoke of their son, of their grief and unending love, and Caleb took to the stage, singing an acoustic version of a song that he had written for Sam, not ashamed at the tears that fell down his cheeks. The service had been a wonderful way to say goodbye to Sam, and Caleb felt that he had finally been laid to rest properly.

The mourners headed to Piccolo's bar and café after the service for lunch, a favourite haunt of the entire Roman family. Caleb took a moment before the food was served to check his mobile phone, seeing two text messages, one from Maria and one from Gabby. He skimmed Maria's first, smiling as he read it.

Nico and I are thinking of you today x

Caleb's breath caught as he opened the text message from Gabby.

I know today will be hard for you Caleb, just remember this: it is not your fault, none of it. Also, make sure you take care of yourself today.

Caleb's heart soared. Gabby had remembered what day it was, what the date was, although there was no way for her to have known about the memorial service specifically, she had known that he would be struggling today and she had reached out to him. maybe there was hope for them after all. For now, it was enough for Caleb.

The rest of the week passed in much the same way as the start of the week, with Caleb and the Three Odd Lizards taking part in a series of interviews with the local television networks as well as a role as guest hosts on a popular game show. Caleb and the Three Odd Lizards spent all of Thursday and most of

Friday holed up in the recording studio, getting their newest single recorded and mixed for the radio, ready for a Saturday release, and then on Friday night Caleb and the Three Odd Lizards were guests of honour at a charity event promoting and fundraising for the Children's Unicorn Charity, an organisation that grants wishes to seriously and terminally ill children. The Three Odd Lizards had been strong supporters of the charity ever since it was first founded by Alex's parents, Sarah and David, over twenty years ago when their youngest child, Abby, had been diagnosed with a rare form of cancer. After a particularly cruel battle, Abby had thankfully made a full recovery and had now been in remission for almost fifteen years.

Saturday dawned way too early for Caleb, the Three Odd Lizards meeting at Caleb's house before travelling together to a local network radio station to give an interview and exclusively release their new single. The debut was insane, with rows and rows of fans lining the streets for a chance of a closer look at Caleb and Three Odd Lizards. After the interview Caleb, Alex, and Nate walked the crowds, signing autographs and happily posing for photographs. The boys were always euphoric after a great launch, and they travelled back to Caleb's house on a wave of success and excitement. They said goodbye in the driveway, embracing each other firmly, Caleb eager to get moving and to enact the final phase of his plan to win Gabby back. With his friend's well wishes ringing in his ears, Caleb pulled out of his driveway, and with a toot of his horn, slid into the busy Sydney traffic, headed for Beryl Creek.

CHAPTER TWENTY-THREE

Caleb stepped into the bakery, narrowly avoiding being taken out by a woman rushing past with an armload of pastries. He heard her call out triumphantly to a small crowd gathered nearby, who sent up a collective cheer as she laid her loot down on the table in front of them. The business was indeed booming. He could see Gabby from here, smoothly directing a staff member while ringing up another order. He wanted her to look up, to notice him, to smile in recognition, but she was too busy to notice another customer, let alone him, standing at the back of the store. He cleared his throat and called out confidently "Gabby." He could hear the gasps, the rustles, the whispers, saw the heads whipping around as people identified him, recognised him in the crowd. It was unfair of him, he knew that, but he wasn't above using the crowd to his advantage. The Three Odd Lizards had dropped their newest single yesterday, a chart-topper all the stations had declared, and speculation was rife over the choice of the title, *Gabby's Song*. Now at least, for the fans in the bakery, that question had been answered.

The crowd parted as Caleb made his way slowly up to the counter, walking around it slowly, giving Gabby a chance to flee if she chose to. He came to a stop in front of her, resting a hand on the small of her back and urging her forward, closing the distance between them. "Gabby." His eyes never left hers.

"Caleb." Her voice was unsure, questioning. Slowly, ever so slowly, Caleb lowered his head, bringing his lips down on hers,

Gabby's eyes fluttered shut, a soft moan escaping as Caleb deepened the kiss, her hands snaking up his back and around his head. It was dizzying, disorientating. A cheer erupted, someone wolf-whistled. Caleb felt Gabby tense up, turned her in his arms slightly so that she was shielded from the prying eyes of the crowd. He guided her out into the kitchen, shutting the door behind them without a backwards glance.

Under the harsh glare of the kitchen lights, Gabby returned to her senses, rounding on Caleb, and crossing her arms angrily over her chest. "What on earth was that? what are you doing here?"

"That, darling, was a kiss," Caleb answered lightly, ignoring her anger, "and I am here for you. I would have thought that was obvious."

"Go to hell Caleb," Gabby spat, turning away from Caleb, but not before he saw tears on her cheeks.

"Gabby, what happened? What's wrong?" He placed his hands on her shoulders, turning her to him.

"Nothing is wrong Caleb, honestly, you came all this way for nothing, I'm sorry. Mum shouldn't have called you in the first place, I told her not to, I told her it would just be a false alarm." Gabby was muttering more to herself than Caleb at this stage.

"Gabby, what on earth does your mum have to do with this? Why would she call me? Is everything okay with your dad?"

"Hmm? Oh, yes, dad is fine." Gabby sighed, not quite meeting Caleb's eyes. "I had a bit of a stomach flu, that is all, mum panicked, as she usually does."

"Okay," Caleb drew the word out, not quite sure what the flu had to do with her mother calling him. Unless…" Gabby, what exactly are you saying?" Caleb didn't dare to hope. "Are you pregnant?" His voice is barely a whisper.

"No," Gabby sighed deeply. "I thought I was, but don't worry Caleb, I am not going to trap you into anything, it turns out it was just a false alarm, I'm not pregnant after all." Did she sound disappointed? Was it possible that she wanted to be pregnant to him, was it possible that Gabby actually wanted to have his baby? A wide smile spread across Caleb's face, her mother was right, she did love him.

"Gabby, I'm sorry," he drew her into his arms, holding her tightly. "I'm so sorry that I lied to you, I'm sorry that you didn't trust me enough to reach out when you thought you were pregnant."

"You are?" Gabby looked up at him, frowning, feeling as if she was really seeing him for the first time.

"Yes, desperately sorry. If there was a way that I could take it all back, I would."

"You don't have to do that Caleb, I overreacted, I was too sensitive. You had every right to protect your privacy, it is me who is sorry." Gabby conceded.

"I should have told you the truth before we spent the night together, I'm sorry for that Gabby, do you think you can forgive me?"

"If you forgive me?"

"What on earth do you need to apologise for?"

"It wasn't that I didn't trust you, that was not why I didn't tell you that I thought that I might be pregnant with your child."

"It wasn't?"

"No. I thought, I mean, I wasn't sure how you would react. I thought you would be angry, that you wouldn't believe me, that you would leave again, or worse, that you might actually ask me to get rid of it." Gabby finished in a whisper, afraid of making eye contact.

"Planned or not Gabby, that would never be an option for me, do you understand?" Gabby nodded silently. "I'm truly sorry, I should have been there when you found out, it won't happen again, I promise. Next time I will be there every step of the way."

"There will be a next time?" Gabby sounded confused.

"Of course," Caleb replied confidently. "I was thinking two, maybe three more children. Unless you would like more?" He smiled down at her.

"I'm sorry, I feel like I may have missed something. You want to have children?"

"Yes."

"With me?"

"Yes."

"Why?" Gabby really was confused now.

"Because I love you," Caleb replied, as if it was the most obvious thing in the world.

"You love me?" Gabby sounded incredulous. She reached down and pinched herself on the arm, hard, to make sure that she wasn't dreaming, that she really was awake.

"I do." Caleb grinned at her confusion. "Did you watch any of the morning television programmes yesterday? Or even today?"

"No", Gabby shook her head.

"Oh," Caleb sounded defeated. "Well," he perked up, "I wrote you a song, it is actually the newest single released by my band the Three Odd Lizards. I sat down and wrote it in a night, I am writing again Gabby, it is as if a weight has been lifted off my shoulders. We recorded it last week, and debuted it yesterday, otherwise I would have come straight here, for you. I left as soon as I could, I drove all night, I stayed overnight in Bradford, in our hotel, I took a room for the week, I wasn't sure you would see me. The song is good Gabby, it released well and charts everywhere have it at number one, which is nice, but I wrote it for you, I want you to hear it, will you let me sing it to you Gabby?"

At her nod, he sat down on a kitchen stool and began. "I said something stupid and lost the girl that I love, come back to me baby, it will be different, cross my heart. I loved you forever, I just didn't know, took me lying to come to find you. Cast out, forgotten, drowning in death, no words, no music, silence at its best." Caleb took a deep breath before continuing. "A sundress blowing in the wind, the feel of my hand on your skin. A dream? Heaven? A weird kind of hell? I just want you; can you tell? White picket fence, babe at your breast, entwined, one heart beats in your chest. Lamenting, repenting, storing the doubt away, I buried it all, laid it in the ground today. The sun was shining, clouds all disappeared, a single word, come on, it is all I need to hear. I'll beg if you want me to, get down on one knee, spend a lifetime proving it, you belong with me." He looked at Gabby, she looked at him, tears shimmered in her eyes.

"You wrote me a song?" Gabby sounded incredulous, Caleb wasn't sure if she had liked it or not.
"Yes." He nodded.
"Why?"
"Because I love you, and that is the kind of thing that a guitarist does when he is in love with a girl," Caleb answered simply.

154

"Really?" Gabby still didn't sound convinced.

"Of course," Caleb stated.

"How many songs have you written?" Gabby wanted to know, needed to know.

"For a girl or in general?" Caleb wasn't sure what the parameters were.

"In general." Gabby decided to start with the largest number.

"Eight hundred and forty-three." Caleb knew without having to think about it.

"Okay, how many of those were for girls?"

"One," Caleb smiled, knowing exactly what it was that Gabby was asking.

"Just one?"

"Yes, this one," Caleb pointed at her.

"This one?"

"Yes, this one, this song, this girl," Caleb clarified.

"Why?" Gabby pushed.

"Because I love you. I think you'll find it pretty easy to understand if you say it a few times, want to try saying it back to me?" Caleb stepped closer to Gabby.

"You love me?" Gabby reiterated.

"Yes." Caleb tilted her head upwards.

"You really love me?" Gabby honestly could not believe it.

"Yes."

"Me?"

"Yes, you. And Sofia and Lucia of course." Caleb added.

"Okay then." Gabby nodded in agreement.

"Okay then?" Now it was Caleb's turn to be confused.

"Yes, okay then, I love you too," Gabby said, smiling widely up at Caleb's stunned expression.

"You love me?" Caleb said the words slowly, letting them sink in.

"Yes Caleb, I love you. I have loved you since that night underneath the peppercorn tree," Gabby said softly, placing her hand on Caleb's cheek. "I knew there was something vulnerable, special, about you. I would never have agreed to go to Bradford with you if I had any doubts about my feelings for you." It was all that Caleb needed to hear, in a single move he brought his mouth down on Gabby's, tilting her chin to deepen the kiss, loving the way she felt as she melted against him. reluctantly he pulled away with a groan.

"Gabby, we can't," Caleb groaned. "I want to, obviously I want to," Caleb chuckled, in no doubt to the fact that Gabby could very well feel just how much he wanted to through the thin fabric of his jeans. "But we can't, at least, not here." He smiled ruefully at her.

"I know," Gabby gripped his shirt in her balled-up fists, resting her forehead on his chest. "But the drive to Bradford is ever so long." She whispered.

"You little minx," Caleb laughed, "you have a bakery to run, and I need to see your father".

"I have a small staff now," Gabby started proudly, "I am sure they can cope without me for a few hours."

"I can't wait to hear all about it, I feel as if I have been gone for years instead of only a couple of weeks". He kissed her lightly on the forehead. "Go, tell your staff that you are leaving, I'll wait."

Gabby was back in moments, bag slung over her shoulder, looping her arm through Caleb's. "I'm ready," she nodded, sharing a brilliant smile with him, knowing that he had parked his car out the front of the bakery and that it meant passing through the throng of his fans. The cheers started as soon as they opened the kitchen door, with everyone chanting Gabby's name in unison, a deafening crescendo.

"Caleb," a young fan screamed, "did you get the girl?" Caleb looked at Gabby and smiled.

"Yes, I got my girl." He announced, as a deafening cheer went up in the bakery. "Try Gabby's tiramisu while you are here, it should be world-famous," he declared as Gabby drew him out of the front door and onto the street. Despite what Caleb had said about needing to talk to her father, he turned left onto the highway, Gabby giggling with delight when she realised that they were headed towards Bradford after all.

CHAPTER TWENTY-FOUR

The door barely shut behind them, Caleb wasted no time in closing the distance between them, claiming her mouth with a hard kiss, desire blazing in his eyes. There were no sweet words, no gentle teasing touches, only a raw, primal need to touch, to taste, to feel. Caleb spun with Gabby in his arms, pushing her up against the lounge room wall, his hands sought out the hem of her dress, sliding it up her thighs slowly, bunching it at either side of her waist. He broke their kiss momentarily to rip her dress up and over her head, carelessly throwing it on the floor beside them. He bowed his head in reverence, in awe, his eyes darting back and forth, soaking in every single inch of Gabby's skin, committing it all to memory, never wanting to forget for even one single second what she looked like.

He dipped his head to her breast, capturing it in his mouth, suckling it through the lacy confines of her bra, the combination of the fabric and his tongue sending shockwaves of pleasure shooting through Gabby.

"Caleb, oh my god, yes, Caleb, please." Gabby bit out, writhing beneath Caleb's mouth, twisting her hips in an effort to get closer to him, to have him get closer to her. Caleb heeded her cries, sliding his fingers around to her back, unclasping her bra, watching delightedly as her breasts sprang free of their confines.

"You are so gorgeous, so utterly gorgeous," he crooned to her before seizing her breast again, nipping and sucking on one while his free hand kneaded the other breast, rolling and tweaking her nipple between his thumb and finger, delighting in her gasps and moans.

Gabby slid her hands down Caleb's chest, her fingers finding the buttons on his jeans, slim fingers unpopping each button one at a time, torturously slowly, before pushing them down to his knees along with his boxer shorts. Her eyes drank him in, he was already rock hard, his length bulging, twitching, pulsing with need, for her. Gabby slowly drew a finger down Caleb's length, causing him to jerk, his member dancing with her hand, his engorged head nudging her thigh. In one fluid movement Caleb captured Gabby's hands, bringing them above her head and holding them there, drawing one of Gabby's legs up to rest on his hip, Caleb used his fingers to shove Gabby's panties to one side, plunging into her wetness with a grunt.

Caleb felt Gabby stretch to accommodate his size, loving the way that he was able to fill her so completely. Angling Gabby's hips, he withdrew his length fully before plunging inside her again, deeper and deeper, increasing his speed with each thrust. He knew that she was close; he saw it in her eyes as his length plundered as deep inside her as was physically possible. With a final thrust, he tipped her over the edge. Her eyes wide, Gabby clawed at his chest, panting fast, dripping with need, lost in screams of pleasure and the heady scent of lust. Watching her come undone was all that he needed, and with a triumphant shout, his orgasm ripped through him. They clung to each other, not daring to move, until their breathing returned to normal.

Giddy with life, Caleb scooped Gabby up into his arms and carried her through to the bedroom, his traitorous member already gearing up for an encore. Placing Gabby carefully onto the bed as if she were made of glass, Caleb simply stood and looked, drinking her all in. He wondered if he would ever tire of looking at her? Gabby looked up at Caleb through lowered lashes and smiled. Slowly, very slowly, he leant down and captured Gabby's mouth in a kiss that was so full of love and longing that it left her in no doubts as to his feelings for her and brought tears to her eyes.

"I love you." He stated simply, looking into her eyes.

"I love you too," she replied with certainty.

"Gabby," Caleb shifted his weight, pushing himself off of the bed, heading to the door. "Don't move, I will be right back." He padded through to the lounge room, reaching down to collect his pants from where he had dropped them on the floor, putting his hand into his pocket to retrieve the item he had stowed there before he had left home yesterday, returning to Gabby and offering her the open ring box. "Gabby, I love you. I have loved you since you told me that my cupcake wasn't completely terrible, I think I might have always loved you, that I might have been born to love you, only you, for the rest of my life. Gabby, will you marry me?"

"Yes Caleb, I will." For Caleb, it felt as if Gabby's answer had come through on megaphones, carried in neon lights. She was his, she was really his, now and forever.

Caleb slid the ring onto Gabby's finger, a stunning diamond and sapphire creation that had been Caleb's grandmother's, that he had had altered especially for Gabby. It looked good on her finger, like it belonged there, which it did. Gabby smiled at him, drew him down into a kiss, her hands wantonly sliding down to grasp his balls, leisurely rolling them in her hands as he deepened the kiss, shifting slightly so that she had a better angle. Caleb moaned into her mouth, biting down on her lip as his member spasmed and twitched in anticipation. Unable to wait any longer, Gabby broke away from Caleb, pushing off the bed with a soft thud, kneeling on the floor in front of him, and pushing his legs open wider, nestling herself between them.

Starting at the base of Caleb's thick length, Gabby gripped firmly, slowly pulling down, all the way until the end, before slowly pushing her fist back up his shaft, again and again, using her free hand to massage his aching balls, twisting and pulling them slightly, listening to the way that she was able to make Caleb moan. With a saucy wink at Caleb, she placed her hands on his knees, and took his stiff length into her waiting mouth, her soft moistness waiting for him. she started slowly, licking and nibbling, slowly biting her way down his shaft, the tastiest popsicle she had ever eaten, one that she knew she would come back for time and time again without ever getting bored of the flavour.

Pulling back, she kissed his swollen head, taking him into her mouth slowly, all the way, deeper and deeper, watching his eyes widen as his length disappeared inside her throat. When he was fully encased inside her mouth, she started suckling, harder and harder, watching his eyes start to glaze over, hearing his fevered mutterings of her name, his grunted promises of payback, his frantic begging for release. She bobbed up and down along his shaft, faster and faster, she knew he was close, felt herself getting wetter at the prospect of his orgasm, knowing that she had this power over him, that she could reduce him to a quivering mass, was a heady thing. With a triumphant shout, Caleb came, filling Gabby's mouth with his juices, praising her to the heavens. She licked him clean as he watched her through hooded eyes, before rejoining him on the bed, kissing him lightly.

With a lazy smile, Caleb's hand slid up Gabby's thigh, finding her sweet spot, pushing her folds gently out of the way to reach her bundle of nerves. She was so wet for him, because of him, the thought delighted him, Caleb could already feel himself starting to grow hard again. He would never have thought it possible, this kind of stamina, not in his thirties in any case, and yet, with Gabby he was insatiable. He wondered if the day would ever come when he would be bored with how wet he could make her, if he would ever tire of her being so ready to receive him. He cupped her mound, his thumb idly circling her nub, Gabby moaning softly beside him. He raised himself up on one elbow, looking down at Gabby, her face flushed from their lovemaking.

With a contented sigh, Caleb dipped his head to capture her breast, teasing her nipple until he felt it harden and pebble beneath his tongue, suckling and biting, loving the sounds it elicited from Gabby, committing it all to memory. He loved discovering just what it was that made her come undone and loses her senses. His fingers slid down Gabby's body, dipping into her silky folds, plunging in and out with a leisurely speed, as Gabby moaned and writhed beneath him. Caleb released her breast reluctantly, the pinkened bud swollen from his suckling, a beacon beckoning him back, urging him to return. Caleb moved slowly down Gabby's body, leaving a trail of kisses and nibbles as he went, lower and lower, until he reached her core.

He flicked his tongue over her sensitive bud, her hips jerked beneath him. raising himself to his knees, Caleb placed his hands on her thighs, urging them apart, further, as far apart as they would go. He wanted to, needed to, see all of Gabby, the sight of her fully open, for him, knowing that she was his alone, had his member standing erect, painfully hard, waiting, twitching to be back inside of her again. Caleb bent his head, resting his hands gently on the inside of Gabby's thighs, keeping her wide open, his tongue probed deep into her very core, teasing, tasting, drinking in her juices, as she bucked her hips beneath him, her breathing growing laboured, begging Caleb for release.

Caleb pulled back abruptly, leaning over her and driving his erection into her without warning, before pulling out fully and driving in again. Gabby screamed out in surprise, in pleasure, her walls stretching to accommodate Caleb's thickness and length, loving the way he filled her. Gabby arched her back and bucked her hips to meet his powerful thrusts, screaming his name, again and again, a mantra, a prayer on her lips, as he drove in harder and deeper, his thick member filling her to breaking point, his pelvic bone rubbing against her sensitive bundle of nerves, shooting rivers of pleasure through her with each of his powerful thrusts. Gabby held nothing back as Caleb moved within her, she was his completely, and he was hers, they moved as one, in unison.

Pulling his hardened length out fully, Caleb gave one final thrust all the way into Gabby's welcoming core, and felt her walls tighten around his stiffened member as he pushed her over the edge, hearing her scream out his name with wild abandon. With one final thrust he exploded inside her, gripping her hips for support, until totally spent, he collapsed beside her.

CHAPTER TWENTY-FIVE

The way the water sluiced down Gabby's body to splash off of her puckered nipples was mesmerising, Caleb following the droplet with his eyes until it disappeared between her thighs. He caught the next droplet on his tongue, following the trail it would have taken with his mouth, his tongue pushing through Gabby's damp folds to plunge deep inside her core. He didn't care that they were supposed to be showering, that they were meant to be getting ready to head back to Beryl Creek, he had no idea just how the sight of Gabby in the shower would affect him. His hands wrapped around her buttocks, steadying her, he lifted one of her legs up onto his shoulder, giving his mouth unfettered access to her core. As his tongue flicked in and out, Gabby stopped pretending to be actually showering, arching her back and encouraging him with moans.

With a hard twist of her sensitive nub, she orgasmed for him, her juices running over his tongue, dribbling down her thigh. He licked her up eagerly, loving the way she tasted in his mouth, before nibbling his way up her thigh and across her stomach before finally settling his mouth on her nipple, biting, and twisting it between his teeth. Gabby was already quivering in anticipation, unwilling to linger, Caleb crushed her body to his, capturing her bottom lip between his teeth, biting down gently before sucking. He placed his hand where his tongue had just been, kneading and massaging, feeling her dripping wetness mixed with the shower water, her core pulsing with desire.

Leaving his hand there, cupping her sex, he trailed his mouth down to her breast, latching onto it, suckling until her nipple puckered inside his mouth, rolling the hardened nib around his mouth, flicking it with his tongue, nipping at it with his teeth as Gabby arched her back and steadied herself on the shower wall, whimpering his name in desperation. Breaking away from her with a ragged breath, his erection jutting out proudly for all to see, Caleb lifted Gabby up, anchoring her back on the shower wall, sliding her down his hardened length and tethering her to him. His stiff member twitched and jerked inside of Gabby, content to be home. Gabby gasped as Caleb stabbed into her, his length always surprised her. As she clung to him, clutching his broad shoulders for support, his generous length grew even longer still as he stabbed into her shaking core again and again. Their release, when it came, was explosive, rolling spasms that anchored him inside her, their mutual shouts of triumph filling the air around them.

Eventually, they showered, dressing slowly, delaying the inevitable. They drove back to Beryl Creek in silence, sharing a secret smile. They swung past Lucia and Sofia's school, surprising them both, their innocent chatter lighting up the car ride home. Caleb was greeted like family by both Nico and Maria, who hugged him warmly and shed a few tears as she welcomed him to the family. Gabby proudly showed off her engagement ring, Lucia, and Sofia clamouring over it and begging to be her flower girls. Caleb made a phone call home to his parents, putting them on to speakerphone so that everyone could hear their overjoyed reactions. Nate and Alex were next, happily congratulating the couple and already starting to plan Caleb's bachelor party.

They spent the evening making plans as a family, both Caleb and Gabby keen to include everyone. There were a lot of plans to be made, and a lot of decisions to finalise, especially in relation to Lucia and Sofia and the bakery. The easiest decision also ended up being the hardest. With only eight weeks left of the school year, it was agreed that Gabby would remain in Beryl Creek with Lucia and Sofia, and the three of them would travel to join Caleb in Sydney in the middle of December. On the weekends that Caleb was unable to travel to Beryl Creek, Gabby would take the girls out of school at lunchtime on the Friday and they would travel to Sydney, returning by Monday lunchtime. With everything else that had to be organised, the time would certainly fly, and the sacrifice would be worth it to allow Lucia and Sofia to finish the school year with their friends.

CHAPTER TWENTY-SIX

Laughing, Caleb turned to look at Sam, his eyes twinkling. "See," he couldn't help teasing the other man, "I knew you would have a good time tonight Sammy."

"I always have a good time with you little brother," Sam ruffled Caleb's perfectly lacquered hair, deliberately squashing the rock star 'ruffled fresh from bed' style that Caleb had spent hours perfecting earlier that night. "But we can't all be irresponsible rockstars now can we, Callie?" Sam used the childhood nickname he knew Caleb detested so much, knowing it would get a rise out of him. "Some of us actually have to work to earn a living!" It was the same banter that always existed between them, the ribbing and poking fun that was laced with the love that comes from being part of a family.

"Work?!" snorted Caleb, "Ha! As if! You're a partner in a law firm Sammy, how much work can you possibly do? Don't you have a staff of people all waiting to jump to your command?" Caleb's raucous laugh mingled with Sam's deep chortle.

"Staff? That's your department brother dear, how many do you have now? Eighteen? Ninete-"

"Watch out!" Caleb's panicked shout interrupts Sam, and he blinks once, surprise etching his features. The unrelenting screech of bare metal tyre rims on bitumen reaches a crescendo before fading into silence, the world turning black, the only sound an incessant beep, beep, beep.

"Caleb? Caleb? Caleb, are you even listening to me?" Caleb turned around slowly, not trusting his ears, it can't be, can it?

"Sam?" He whispered, a lump in his throat, not daring himself to speak aloud.

"Of course, it is me Caleb, who else would it be?" Concern etched Sam's features. "Caleb, are you feeling alright?"

"I…How are you here?"

"You deserve this Caleb, don't ever doubt that. Gabby loves you, she will keep loving you, until all breath has left her body. That is what I came to say, to tell you. I am so proud of you, I always have been. Gabby and the girls, your new baby, you were always meant to be a family."

"I miss you." Caleb choked out.

"I know." Sam replied, "It isn't fair, is it? You aren't going to see me anymore Caleb, after today you won't have these nightmares anymore."

"What? No, Sam that-"

"You will still remember me, Caleb, and every time you look at your son you will know I am there, but no more late-night conversations, it isn't fair. You need to let me go now, Caleb."

"I can't, Sam, I just can't."

"Yes, you can, you are so much more than you give yourself credit for. I love you, Caleb, I was always so proud to be your brother."

"Sam, I love you." Tears rolled down Caleb's cheeks unnoticed.

"I know." Sam fixed Caleb with his trademark grin, winked, then turned and left the room. Caleb sat bolt upright, sunlight streaming through the open window, the blue haze of the ocean glistening outside. He felt calmer than he had in months, more peaceful, more like himself.

"Goodbye Sam," he whispered into the empty room, before climbing out of bed and heading downstairs in search of the smell of coffee currently permeating his house.

He found his father in the kitchen, along with Nate, Tom, and Alex, the four of them attempting to decipher the instruction manual for the barista machine.

"Here," Caleb stepped into the kitchen, pressed a few buttons, and stepped back, watching as the machine sprang to life, hissing and spitting.

"Huh," his dad commented, "I didn't realise you knew how to make this thing work."

"Dad, please, I know a thing or two about my own kitchen."

"Gabby showed you huh?" His dad guessed correctly, chuckling as he handed Caleb a cappuccino.

"Thanks, dad, everything all set?" Caleb tried not to let his nerves get the better of him.

"All set," his father confirmed.

Caleb couldn't settle, he fidgeted with his suit, he paced up and down the lounge room, he got on everyone's nerves. Eventually, Nate, Tom, and Alex had had enough, the three of them ganging up and ushering Caleb into the music studio, placing a guitar into his hands and telling him to sit there and play until they came back for him. seriously, they shook their heads, if this was love, they were glad they were single. By the time the guys had everything else sorted out and returned to tell Caleb it was time to go, he had completely written a new song, brandishing it at them, excitedly telling them that this song was the one, this song was the one that he and Gabby should share their first dance as husband and wife to, and would they please play it for him. at their agreeance, he clapped them all on their backs and strode from the room heading for the cars.

Gabby looked exquisite, her Grace Kelly inspired wedding gown flattered her figure perfectly, complimenting the soft blush of her cheeks. Her parents had left her alone, taking Lucia and Sofia downstairs to wait. Gabby looked at her reflection in the floor-length mirror, smoothing out the fabric of the dress, marvelling at the way it hung, the feel of it beneath her fingers. Lowering her veil, she gave her reflection a nod, before heading downstairs to join the rest of her family. Sofia and Lucia waited patiently, they looked so pretty in their matching sage green bridesmaids' dresses, her mother gasping and bursting into tears when she saw Gabby.

"Oh, you look so beautiful!" Her mother embraced her, kissing her cheeks.

"I'm ready," Gabby spoke to the room, her father nodding proudly. "Let's go."

The church was glittering, Caleb had insisted that Gabby should have the wedding she had always wanted, her dream wedding, no matter how outrageous or what the cost was. The wooden pews had been decorated with bunches of eucalyptus leaves mixed with stems of delicate teardrop crystals. The same crystals had been used to hang from the ceiling like bunting, and the girls both wore subtle tiaras from the same designer. Maria fussed with straightening Sofia and Lucia's dresses, Nico offering Gabby his arm, walking now with the aid of a cane. As the music started and Lucia and Sofia began their walk down the aisle, Gabby turned to her father and smiled, kissing him on the cheek softly.

Gabby couldn't keep her eyes off Caleb waiting at the other end of the aisle, she could hardly believe that he was hers, that she was actually about to marry him, to become Mrs Roman. She would never in a million years have thought that she would ever marry a rockstar, or marry at all if she was being honest, yet here she was, about to embark on her greatest adventure with her best friend and lover, a man who she would give her life for, a man who she knew she could not live without, who she didn't want to live without. If it had not been for her father's steady walk, she would have run down the aisle to join him.

Caleb wore a tailored suit, having told Gabby that he would be retiring his all-black wardrobe, with the exception of his skinny black jeans, which he would keep, for her eyes only. As Gabby drew closer to Caleb, she took a moment to look around at all of the people who had come so far to celebrate their day. It seemed as if everyone who had been able to get to Sydney had come, with guests flying in from as far away as Dubai, Canada, and even London. Nearly the entire town of Beryl Creek had come to Sydney for their special day, feeling especially honoured to be included in their special day. Gabby's and Caleb's family sat together, there were no sides in this wedding, everyone was one family now, their tears and happy faces telling the couple just how happy they were that this day was here at last, just as they had told them both often in the past few months just how blessed they felt that they had found each other.

Standing in front of their family and friends, Caleb and Gabby pledged to love, support, and encourage each other, until death do they part, a promise that they kept for the rest of their days. Much later, as Caleb and Gabby shared their first dance as husband and wife, to a song that he had written with her in mind, a song that would later reach platinum status on the billboards, Gabby guided Caleb's hand to her still flat stomach with a secret smile, whispering in his ear that she suspected that in six months their family may be about to grow bigger. Caleb stopped suddenly, eyes round, asking her if she was sure. At her delighted nod, he picked her up, swinging her around with a whoop, before placing her down gently and kissing her with a passion only she would ever know.

EPILOGUE

Gabby's hospital room had been as busy as Pitt Street, with dozens of well wishes keen to stop by and to congratulate the new parents and to try and get a peek of their sweet baby. Caleb had been fiercely protective of Gabby throughout the entire pregnancy, insisting on hiring a bodyguard for her, just in case fans of the Three Odd Lizards got a little too close for comfort. Gabby had told him not to overreact, that she would be fine, and she had been. She did relent however and agree to a bodyguard at the hospital after she was admitted with Braxton hicks and a fan snuck in masquerading as a doctor. She was only thankful that she was fully clothed, and that Caleb had been running late that day, otherwise things might have been vastly different.

Caleb was relishing his new role of daddy, fussing over his pregnant wife, who he claimed had never looked more beautiful, and spending time making sure that Lucia and Sofia knew that they were loved and special. The adoption papers had finally come through, and Caleb was now listed as Lucia and Sofia's legal father, the knowledge of which gave him great peace. The girls had taken to Sydney with an amazing fervour, the private school Gabby and Caleb enrolled them in offered a range of classes, and both girls easily found their niche. Lucia had discovered a passion for art and was excelling at the subject. Caleb and Gabby had been happy to encourage her, even installing a studio at the back of the property so that she could continue her creative pursuits during the school holidays.

Sofia on the other hand had picked up a cello during their tour of the school, fingering the bow longingly, hesitantly confessing on the car ride home that she might like to learn how to play. The schoolteacher personally phoned Gabby after Sofia's first lesson, informing her that as far as she was concerned, Sofia had real talent and that she needed to be given a cello and professional lessons without delay. Gabby baulked at the cost, but Caleb insisted that the most important thing they would ever do was to encourage the girls in their passions. Sofia's cello was delivered the following day, now six months later and the change in her was incredible, listening to her was pure joy, she had such an infinity with the instrument.

Nico and Maria had become firm friends with Peter and Judy and were loving retirement. Caleb and Gabby had purchased the bed and breakfast and the bakery from her parents, intending to keep them both, at least until the girls were older. Gabby had hired a full-time staff for the bakery, four bakers and six shop assistants, and after Caleb's paparazzi endorsement of the bakery, and subsequent leaking of the fact that he was now, technically, co-owner, the business had boomed and had not slowed down. Nico and Maria had moved to Sydney shortly after Caleb and Gabby's wedding, and Caleb had bought them a modest single storey house in Double Bay, a short drive from both Caleb and Gabby, and Peter and Judy. The house had five bedrooms, a swimming pool for Nico's therapy, and a lovely entertaining area, ideal for when the grandchildren came to stay.

For now, though, Gabby's room was filled with family only, Tom, Nate, and Alex having just left. As Caleb gazed down at his son sleeping in his arms, he was struck by how lucky he was, how truly blessed to have found Gabby and her family, his family now. Gabby's hospital room was full of flowers, it looked like a florist had opened up shop, a testament to just how many people cared about Gabby and how many people wished them well.

"Caleb?" Gabby touched his arm.

"Yes love," Caleb tore his eyes away from his son to look at his wife of six months.

"You don't have to hold him constantly you know," she teased him gently, "you can put him down, he will be fine in the bassinette."

"Not a chance," Caleb grinned at Gabby. "This is my son," Caleb choked up as he said the words, "I don't want to miss anything." His son, honestly, Caleb could not believe it. He looked around the room, at his parents and at his daughters, Lucia and Sofia, at Nico and Maria, each one of them loving him, loving Gabby, without question. Sam was right, it had always meant to be. He cleared his throat and spoke directly to his sleeping son. "Samuel Nicolas, you are named after two of the finest people your mama and I ever loved. Welcome home little one, you are wanted, you are treasured, and you are loved."

THE END

About The Author

An international bestselling and award-winning author of sweet contemporary romance, Kathleen's novels showcase thought-provoking plots and strong emotions that have been likened to a Hallmark movie. Featuring feisty heroines and strong heroes, where everyone gets a happily ever after. To discover more about Kathleen: Connect on social media

Read More of Kathleen's Books

THE SURGEON'S BABY Sample

The door to the clinic burst open, a frantic Emma rushing through to the reception desk, her heart leaping in her throat, her pulse racing with panic. A problem, how can there be a problem? She was told everything was fine, that the procedure had gone to plan, she was flying home tomorrow!

"Emma, Doctor Delaney is expecting you, go straight through," the receptionist waved her hand vaguely in the direction of a hallway and turned back to her magazine. Emma tried to slow her steps, tried to force down the bile she could taste in the back of her mouth.

"Emma dear, come in," Doctor Delaney places a hand on Emma's back and ushers her through the doorway. "Can I get you anything? Tea? Water?"

"Thank you, I'm-" Emma stops mid-sentence as her eyes land on a second person, paused, framed in the doorway.

"Ah," Doctor Delaney follows Emma's gaze, clapping his hands together. "Ivan, come in, take a seat. Emma, this is Doctor Ivan Delgado, Ivan, this is Emma Roberts," he introduces nervously.

Emma's breath caught in her throat as she tried not to stare at Ivan. "Hi" Emma squeaks, her throat like sandpaper, voice wobbling, betraying her nerves.

"I know you must be worried Emma," Doctor Delaney smiles kindly at her, "and I apologise for being cryptic over the telephone, but I felt it was better to have this discussion in private, with all parties concerned." Emma gave herself a mental shake, and leant forward, nodding. "As you know, you requested insemination using an anonymous donor." Doctor Delaney perused her file on the desk in front of him. "I'm very sorry Emma, I'm not sure how to tell you this, but there was a terrible error in our laboratory, our technicians have somehow mixed up the samples. Instead of the anonymous donor you selected, you were mistakenly inseminated with a sample from a private donor, which was meant for storage only."

"I see." Emma's mind raced. What did he mean, a private donor? It was not really that bad, was it? "While I appreciate you telling me this as soon as you became aware of the error, it really makes no difference to me where the sample came from," Emma shrugs, trying to keep calm. "Unless the private donor has a hereditary medical condition, it doesn't change anything."

"Actually," drawls Ivan, leaning back in his chair and crossing his arms over his broad chest, "it changes everything."

"I don't understand, do you work in the lab?" Emma frowned in confusion, turning away from Ivan to face Doctor Delaney. "What exactly are you saying? Is there something wrong with the sample?" Emma was not sure she could stand to find out, the cost of this first procedure had eaten up all of her savings, if it didn't work…Well, she was not sure when, or even if, she would be able to cobble together enough funds to have another attempt.

"No, the sample is medically viable," Doctor Delaney shuffles the paperwork in Emma's file with a pointed look in Ivan's direction, "but it is complicated."

"He means," Ivan interjects dryly, fixing Emma with a scathing look, "that you are having my baby."

"You can't be serious." Emma felt the colour drain from her face as she sat looking from Doctor Delaney to Doctor Delgado and back again, her mouth gaping open.

"I have never been more serious in my life," Ivan's eyes narrow as he watches Emma fidget in her chair. "If you are pregnant, you will be carrying my child, and I expect to be involved every step of the way. Amicably or court-appointed," Ivan shrugged, "I don't care. No child of mine will grow up without their father." The warning in Ivan's voice was clear, and it sent shivers down Emma's spine.

"Emma," Doctor Delaney reaches forward to pat her hand, "it is too early for us to know, but if you are pregnant, Ivan will not only be the father of your baby, but as the two of you have no contract in place, Ivan will have full legal rights to this baby."

End of Sample

www.ingramcontent.com/pod-product-compliance
Lightning Source LLC
Chambersburg PA
CBHW070320120726
47909CB00008B/2524